BEAUTY
SLEEPING

Farha Hasan

SonoBerry Press

DEDICATION

For Nida and Saif

EPIGRAPH

And it is He who takes your souls by night and knows what you have committed by day. Then He revives you therein that a specified term may be fulfilled. Then to Him will be your return; then He will inform you about what you used to do...
Holy Quran 6:60

CHAPTER ONE

The last thing I remember is pricking my finger.

It is the middle of the night. The air is thick and I am covered with beads of perspiration. I awaken abruptly, only to choke on the musky odor of incense. Someone has called out to me. Someone had drawn me out of my steadfast sleep. With bare feet and loose hair, I am consumed by an unknown yearning. It cries out to me; it calls my name…Laila…and I must follow.

At first the sound is weak, like the annoying buzz of a fly, but as I get closer I hear it grow stronger and more rhythmic. The pounding of my heart leads me to a forgotten corridor, a hallway in which there seems no end. My mind implores me to turn back, but my heart will not follow. I listen at every door. Finally, there is but one room left. A hum comes from inside, steady…methodical…purposeful.

Slowly, I open the door to find a fair-haired woman dressed in a delicate, white sari shimmering in the moonlight—too beautiful to be a servant or a seamstress. I feel that I know her. I look more closely. Her hair is pulled back into a bun and shines golden in the moonlight and her face—though not unkind—is focused on her task. The woman concentrates on the wheel that spins, round and round. I am hypnotized by its motion. Sensing my presence, she stops and looks up from her task.

As she looks up, I can tell that she has been waiting for me. She invites me closer. I approach apprehensively until I sit before the contraption, and without a word of instruction I know what to do. Much to my glee, the wheel spins for me. Instinctively, I become a master of the spinning device. I look up in triumph. The woman is speaking, but not to me. It is not the praise I feel I am owed. Her voice is low; her words muddled and undecipherable. The more I listen, the more this murmur resembles a chant—a spell of some sort. She wears a look of triumph.

My vision becomes blurred and then comes the dizziness and a comforting blanket of darkness. Engulfed in blackness, I am aware of what lies on the other side. I can feel the growth, the vines, the shrubs, and the foliage. The growth covers everything in sight, like a cocoon in which I lie like a dormant seed. As it grows, they speak to me. They tell me I will be safe here. I understand now that I am asleep.

CHAPTER TWO

An enchantment crept through the city, it was as subtle and delicate as a mist, but it had eyes and it could see. It had ears and it could hear, and a delicate little tongue that tickled people's ears while threatening to bite. Its urgent whispers persuading, caressing people's hearts until they lost their will and gave in to temptation. First, one person began to yawn, and then another, and so it began...as if touched by a gentle kiss.

The yawning spread throughout the city and people's eyes began to close in the midst of their tasks, from the lowliest street cleaner with broom in hand, to the smart looking doormen in the midst of the very New York City doors they opened. The olive skinned cab drivers yammering in foreign tongues as they collect their fares, and of course the various street vendors, roasting everything from hot dogs, gyros, and shish kebabs, filling the city with their delicious smell.

The merchants in their shops with their fancy dresses and designer purses fell asleep in the midst of displaying their wares. The teachers in their classrooms who stood at podiums nodded off during daily lessons, and of course the kings and queens high in their towering penthouses as they looked upon their kingdom. No one was able to resist the enchantment, and so an entire city fell asleep.

Although engaged in a quiet slumber, they went about their daily lives; walking but unaware of their destination, speaking but unaware of their words, acting but unaware of the performance. Yet, still asleep they would toss and turn thinking that they were awake and their souls wandered aimlessly, cultivating dreams within dreams. They longed to wake-up, but of all the souls who wished for this, there was one in particular whose longing surpassed all others.

I should know. I am asleep and yet still I see my sister; she is curled up in her living room wrapped in a pashmina shawl embroidered in rich, desert colors. She has gone about her life asleep for an unforeseeably long time and now it seems Safia doesn't even want to wake, but she will. For me, she will.

The distant sirens of an ambulance punctuate the silence. It is enough. A soft moan escapes Safia's lips and she stretches, her long legs grazing the arm of the overstuffed couch. Her toes, painted a soft pink, the color of a shy blush, peek out of her comfy, lycra pants. The feel of this foreign fabric against her toes reminds her body that she is not in her own bed. A laptop sits on a coffee table, and surrounding it are swatches of fabric, different colors, textures and patterns that layer one another.

Safia sits up and groggily, rubs her eyes. Without thinking, she reaches for a wad of fabric and then drops it just as suddenly. Ouch! Her thumb is bleeding, a pinprick. *I allow myself a delightful little chuckle.* Safia licks her thumb, sucking on it like a child. She looks at the culprit, a thumbtack, lying on her coffee table rolling aimlessly. It is 2 a.m.; she has crashed without intending to. She had been awake for twenty-four hours. Given her tendency towards insomnia, it's a good thing she lives in a city that never sleeps. She tells herself that she can't remember the last time she slept like a normal person. *I know this is a lie, but to her credit a useful one.*

Gathering her thoughts, Safia runs her finger through her tangled hair and pushes the dark curls behind her ear. She had that dream again, but as she awoke it dissolved into the distance and the last thing she remembered was something brushing against her lips. She looks at her laptop with a hint of a smile. She got it. She had to work all day and all night, but she nailed it. Alerts on her cell phone demand her attention. There are phone messages that she hasn't checked, emails that are pending. She's in no hurry to get back to the real world, and hasn't been for many years.

Stretching out her arms and yawning, Safia gets back into bed. Bouts of sleeplessness have plagued her since her youth. Safia was always trying to fall asleep tossing and turning, while Laila, who slept in the next bed, snored like a hyena, drifting off at a moment's notice. At times even falling asleep mid-sentence while she whispered to Safia, as if a switch had been flipped. It was in these instances that Safia felt the most abandoned. She would close her eyes, count sheep, and try to catch the same enchantment. Finally, she would climb out of bed and sneak out of her room. *I always knew.* Sometimes she snuck into the kitchen to grab a cookie, but more often she would sneak into her grandmother's room. She was always welcome there.

An elderly woman, thin and wiry—always dressed in a pale sari of one cloudy color or another—would be sitting on her prayer mats facing Mecca and holding a tasbeeh, the prayer beads she used when she murmured to herself. Safia would curl up in her grandmother's bed and breathe in the scent of the old woman's blanket, and fall asleep listening to her soft prayers.

It is this memory that Safia takes with her as she finally snuggles into her own bed in her tiny loft. She is alone except for a raggedy stuffed dog with floppy ears that she tugs when she's scared, the lonely drip of a faucet...*and me*. She closes her eyes tightly, hugs the comforter, and remembers her grandmother's voice, the smoothness of her grandmother's sari against her face, and the faint scent of mothballs. This time when she flutters to sleep there are no dreams, only darkness.

CHAPTER THREE

My name, Laila, means night beauty.

This curse is an old one and it has begun again with me. I am asleep and yet I am not. My soul floats somewhere between this world and the next. From overhead I have seen them tend to my body. They have slashed through the jungle and the wreckage. I feel myself in an ambulance, moving down a long road for what seems like a great eternity. The sirens blare. It is jarring and now I crave quiet. I look down at my form. How peaceful it looks. My limbs curled up, a serene expression on my face. I almost look innocent. The old woman…she is long gone.

I realize that I am not stranded. I can fly. There is an invisible umbilical cord connecting me to my body so I can't go far. I zip across the city. I can touch the stars and fly over roof tops. The city is beautiful at night when everyone is dreaming. It is my city. I have laid claim to it. I own it now. Still, I am a little afraid. I am afraid to go too far from my body. Afraid I may not find my way back; afraid of not finding my way home, but I need not worry for it is always there waiting for me. For the first time I begin to listen.

I can hear things, at first it is no more than a soft hum, but then I concentrate and focus and I can understand that they are words, words coming from different people and places that all becomes garbled like a buzzing hive. It takes all my attention to separate the voices, to single out only one, but when I do, I hear it clearly as if eavesdropping on a conversation. It is important that I listen carefully. I must find him. He is the only one who can break this enchantment.

Abruptly, I stop moving. We have arrived at a hospital made from stone, a building with vines climbing up the walls. It is a place that has been asleep for many years. It's been waiting for me.

There is so much more that goes into a structure besides brick and mortar. There is also the essence of the people who inhabit the space. Their collective consciousness seeps into its walls and carries itself from one room to another. Corbette Advertising was housed in the type of building that exuded non-conformity. Some liked to think of it as the place where dreams were made, others of where dreams were sold.

The firm had occupied this piece of psychological real estate for the better part of decades. The upper floors were occupied by beautiful people in beautiful suits, but it was in the basement of the agency, in "the studio" where all the hard labor was done. The basement was where the quirky little elves toiled away the day, often into the better part of the evening. It was where they were free to create their own magical little world and for this they had earned their much deserved reputation.

They were flamboyant fashionistas both male and female and their personalities tended to ooze into the décor, with colorful computers, and bright ads framing its walls. There were also toys on every desk—cartoon characters, mini basketball hoops and candy—not to mention the vibrant ensembles of those who occupied its space. At the back of the studio there was a mini pool table—that no one was supposed to use until after 6 p.m. It was fair to say that the studio, though not a quiet environment, was definitely an enchanted one. So much so in fact, that it had been coined the Dream House—not by its inhabitants who of course didn't much care for labels—but by the suits who occupied the upper echelons of the agency. Whether this term came from a place of wit, amusement, dismay, or a combination of all three was uncertain, but it quickly gained momentum.

Over the years, the studio had become not only Safia's home, but also her place of refuge. The studio's innate quirkiness allowed Safia to feel normal. Ironically, the Dream House had gone a long way to relieve her of a few nightmares, and still Safia was always aware that in the studio she was a bit of an anomaly whose conservative appearance didn't quite match her inner thoughts. It was only in her designs that the fierceness of her personality was allowed to seep through.

It was still early when Safia arrived at work. There had been a flurry of activity since 8 a.m. The graphic designers were either hunched over their computers or stretched out lazily sipping coffee. Safia's cubicle - with its cut outs of magazine ads, color palettes, and even fabric swatches - was her inspiration. In fact, it was indicative of what mades her work so unique, the ability to add the illusion of texture into print.

As she pulled up the campaign she was currently working on, she began to make adjustments, tweaks here and there. Her work was well received by clients and if she kept it up, a promotion to Art Director would be hers. That would lead to her leaving the studio for one of the offices in the Creative Department, something that she both looked forward to and dreaded at the same time.

On a typical day, Safia rarely came up for air before 8p.m. Then, she would stretch out her arms and yawn as if awakening from a deep sleep to which Tyson, the studio's manager, might reply, "Look who's up," and peep over her shoulder to see what she was working on.

Tyson was the one the suits approached when they needed a designer. She assigned projects, followed progress, and reviewed all work with a shrewd eye before it ever left the studio.

When Safia finally took her evening break, she saw Tyson going over drafts with one or more of her designers. Safia too would stretch her legs, walk around the studio, peep into the empty cubicles to look at some of the drafts that were pinned to the wall. If she knew the designer she might post a sticky with a comment, usually a compliment about the use of color or technique.

Last night was such a night. At 9 p.m., stuck on one of her ads, Safia decided to take a break, grab a bite, and see what everyone was doing. When this still did not garner any new insight, she decided to call it quits and go home. Perhaps it was the solitude of the empty subway or the blanket of night or the two hours of late night TV, but Safia's eyes began to flutter and before she knew it, she wasn't there anymore. Safia had fallen into that curious space between wakefulness and sleep. It was only in this space that she could sense her, and their two worlds began to merge, like magic.

She could feel the two realities merge and in the hazy blink of an eye, she began to see images. It was as if someone was speaking to her. At first it was just a snowflake, a shiny gold snowflake, and then two and then two more. They began falling at a dizzying speeds and colors, whirling and whirling like a multi-colored typhoon and now she heard the soft hum that increased into excited frenzy. It was as if their path wasn't random. They were looking for something, for someone. Safia tried to respond but couldn't focus. It all happened too fast. This type of momentum threatened to carry a person over stars and over the night sky. Safia wanted to laugh at the impossibility of it all, drowned in the type of giddiness that comes from extreme tiredness.

When she returned to work, she opened up a file and smiled at her work. The background was lightly dusted with different hues of color, sparkling like diamonds across the page. When she closes her eyes she can see the different particles converge and lift off her page...and with this vision in her mind, Safia presses the send button.

The rest of Safia's day is spent in idleness, jotting down ideas here, doing touch-ups there, strolling around the Dream House, and catching up on office politics and gossip. It is a distraction to keep her from thinking about her doctor's appointment this afternoon. Dr. Wilder makes her feel nervous, unsettled.

One of her friends, a petite girl with short, spiky hair, named Orchid, frets over her design. Safia stops to mull over the concept. There is something about the premise that is not working—a kitschy fifties theme. Orchid's work is usually better than this, but lately she's been distracted. Orchid has always been a wild one—kind of a punkish Tinker Bell—but the last couple of weeks her life has been more turbulent than ever with Tyson having caught her on more than one occasion sneaking in around noon.

"Hey Orchid—rough night yesterday?" Another co-worker, Neal, eyed the dark circles under her eyes. "We missed you. One minute you were here; the next you were gone."

Orchid rolled her eyes and flashed a mischievous smile. "I ditched you to hang out with my old pal, Safe here," giving Safia a wink.

"Don't let that sweet demeanor fool you," continued Orchid, "there's nothing she won't try."

Safia played along. "That's right guys; you need to roll with me more often."

Neal sauntered over. "Where do I sign up?"

Safia looked directly at Neal. It was like looking into a flame—something she usually avoided doing. If anyone could snap her out of a daydream, Neal could. He was the type of guy who worked out six days a week—and it showed. Six-foot-four, clean-shaven, and bald. His form fitting wardrobe tended to be monochromatic in shades of black, white, or gray. Today he wore black leather pants and a white, long-sleeved T-shirt. Coupled with a pair of designer sunglasses, it was enough to carry him from day into evening, not to mention, turn every head in the club regardless if they were male or female. Neal possessed an energy that pulled people in.

Even Safia couldn't help glance up from her cubicle to take a peek. Today she was more than willing to let Neal distract her, to let Orchid pull her into their little clique. Today she could relax. It was tomorrow that she must face the sleepy gray walls of the stone castle and the appointment she dreaded.

Alan Memorial Hospital

There is but one visitor for the young girl in room 7A of the Alan Memorial Hospital and Research Institute. It is an old woman who comes every day, likely her grandmother. The woman is a shrunken little thing with hair piled high into a snow-white bun. Her complexion has become almost translucent, common in women her age. But her most distinctive feature is her voice that does not come out in a whisper the way one would expect, but instead with the volume and richness of an un-tuned instrument, the prelude of an inner melody. It is only her voice now that hints at her hidden strength.

Every day she comes and sits by the girl's bedside with a shawl over her head muttering something in a foreign tongue, but the girl does not stir—nor is she expected to. She sleeps peacefully unaware of her state, undisturbed by the ruckus during the day or the cries during the night and if she has any knowledge of the old woman by her side she does not show it. Still, the woman seems satisfied when she leaves. By now the ritual has become as familiar as any hospital procedure and the old woman as much of a fixture as the girl herself

CHAPTER FOUR

I watch as they lay me down—like a princess.

My hair is loose and I am wearing a white gown. There are tubes coming out of my body and machines to keep me anchored. They bathe me and they comb my hair. Sometimes they talk to me, soothing words, and other times they talk to themselves. I listen. People come to check on me—doctors, nurses, family, and friends. They hold my hand. They whisper prayers. They cry, often blubbering out loud and sometimes whimpering softly. These tears are not lost on me. They remark on how good I look, how lovely, as if I were merely asleep. I am beautiful, I know.

"Laila," they remark, staring down at my figure. "She looks beautiful as always."

My hair is dark, my lips full, thick lashes line my eyes, and my complexion is the color of rich honey. All this seems only to add to their sorrow and my mystique. They feel sad as they leave me alone in my tower. But, I am not alone. They spend a great deal of time sitting with me, watching me. They do not know that as they watch me, I watch them. I can hear their whispers. I can smell their scent, skin mixed with cologne, fast foods, rich pastries, and stale leftovers. It's all there. I can sense their emotions. I can read their thoughts. I whisper in their ears and I speak to them in their dreams. I am the shadow that they do not know is there. I follow them. It is hard not to.

What dull lives they have and yet I envy them. I envy their boring routines, their tedious commutes, and their restless sleep. Most of all, I envy their ability to wake-up...but always too soon, and always before I am done. For when they sleep they come into my world and I speak to them. I speak to them through their dreams and they tell me things. There is something I need to know. There is someone I am looking for, but I can't find him...not without her help.

Aidan has never scaled a castle wall nor slain a dragon in his life. The armor he wears has failed to protect him from life's mishaps, but he's not complaining. Aidan is not heroic in the traditional sense but little does he know, as he awakens at fifty thousand feet drenched in sweat, that his life is about to change. For starters, he should have been feeling like crap. His neck is cramped, his back sore and his muscles tight. It had been that type of night but instead Aidan is feeling surprisingly relaxed.

He smiles at his reflection in the window, a telltale sign he knows he's good looking. If only he were a little more athletic. But he's never raised a shovel in his life, never changed his own tire, and likely couldn't shoot a hoop if his life depended on it. No, he's a numbers guy. He builds models, the type of genius that came to Wall Street right out of school, and helped bring the financial markets to its knees.

It is for this reason that he has the world on his back. It is for this reason that he had just taken the redeye from London to New York, where for three hours he had been listening to his VPs lament the consequences of the bailout—even after so many years—a deal that is both a blessing and a curse. And so Aidan keeps his head down and does his best to blow out the proverbial fires as they flare up in his life. He's grateful for his job and his pitiful bonus. After all, he is at least partially responsible for his firm's failures.

He was not the type to lament his burden, or feel sorry for himself. He knows he's gotten off easy. He still remembers the dark days—and is a little reluctant to let them go—when his old cronies, his bosses, and his bosses' cronies were routinely being crucified in the press. He doesn't know what miracle saved him from complete downfall, but if magic wands exist, one had definitely been used to save his brown ass from going down the drain. There is a new management team in place now and under this new leadership some innovations have taken place.

A more prudent, a more conscientious firm has emerged, at least on the surface. Not the least, but certainly the shittiest is the firm's travel policy, starting with this trip across the pond. He's grateful that he doesn't feel like crap. That's what traveling has come to. Gone are the private jets and caviar with the flight attendants serving gourmet meals—was there ever any doubt. Hell, they were lucky if the firm was willing to spot you a first class ticket, which in his case they weren't.

No fairy godmother could fix that. So Aidan, for the first time in his professional career, has been downgraded to economy. For the first time on a business trip, has had to go through long lines at the airport, INS officers scrutinizing his name, Aidan Musawi, which is a little too Middle Eastern, and his complexion, which is a little too dark for this paranoid post 9/11 climate. He can do nothing else but grin and bear it. His carry-on is searched, his cell phone scrutinized, and his body patted down; just so that he can cram his long legs into a passenger seat with too little leg room, sleep with his neck scrunched to one side, and eat meals that have been genetically engineered to take out all of the flavor.

"I'm too good looking to be a terrorist," he wants to say but he doubts anyone will see the humor. Through no fault of his own he has been blessed with dark unruly locks, steel gray eyes—wolves' eyes—a square jaw, and a height that just grazes six feet. He has that killer smile that makes women weak in the knees, not that it has helped him much. If his professional life is bad, his personal life is worse. He's single or more accurately single again and maybe he wants to keep it that way. He could pull off a decent Prince Charming, but let's face it; he's scared to death of princesses. He has a broken engagement under his belt. It's been two years but it feels like yesterday. He feels its absence hovering over him like a ghost. In truth, he didn't love her all that much, only thinks of her now and then.

What he misses is the guy he used to be. He misses being the star, the boy genius at his company. His misses all the money he made that is dwindling quickly. He misses being that naïve fuck who thought he was invincible. That is, until it all came crashing down, first the economy, then the demotion, and then his engagement. He hasn't gotten around to dating again, although his Pakistani parents keep pressuring him for grandchildren. Outwardly, he likes high-powered women, but secretly he wishes they were a little more like his mother.

Given the stress he's had to endure in the last twenty-four hours he is surprised to be waking up feeling so good, refreshed...like he has just come up from under water. Aidan rubs his face against his pillow. He can still smell her...

Aidan's flight actually lands early and he debates going straight to the office, but thinks better of it. He makes a couple calls, namely his parents—who else would wait up for him? He is grateful for the taxi stand at the airport and that he doesn't have to hail a cab in New York in his grubby state.

When he gets inside the cab the driver is ethnic. Based on his name, Abdul, which is printed on the back of the cab and his complexion, he is either South Asian or Middle Eastern. Middle Eastern, Aidan assess from his accent. Pakistanis tend to roll their r-words a little more. Aidan hopes that the cabbie doesn't try to bond with him. Every now and then when a service person of Muslim background notices his ethnicity there is the inevitable, "What part of the world are you from, Brother?"

He is an American so the question makes him feel a little uncomfortable, white washed—prejudiced even. He feels he has little in common with these cabbies, gas station attendants, and hotel clerks whom share little with him other than the complexion of their skin and a loose affiliation to a religion that is for Aidan more a cultural heirloom than a blueprint for life.

He is relieved that this cabbie is not interested in a conversation. Aidan grabs his cell phone and orders take-out from his favorite place. Hopefully, it will be waiting for him when he arrives. True to their word, he gets a phone call from the front desk not ten minutes after arriving at home.

The delivery guy is here with two chicken shawarma sandwiches smothered in tahini sauce and fries. Greasy food always tastes better late at night. It is 2:00 am. Aidan turns on the Bloomberg channel and digs into his dinner.

CHAPTER FIVE

I have the same dream over and over again.

Every night I walk down the same corridor and every night I know the wheel waits for me at the end, without escape. But now, she is there with me as well. Even the old woman has not forsaken me. She thinks that I have not been listening, but I have. I have listened and I have learned and in doing so, I have become a thief.

I can hold dreams in the palm of my hand. I have learned to capture and play with them, to alter them and send them on their way. There is power in my touch and magic in my breath, even as my body lays mute and helpless, a corpse to all I hold dear. There is a reason that I am here. There is something I must do. How much easier it would be if I weren't still trapped in that wheel, but we must all pay our penance. I can hear my sister's dreams now.

Her dreams interest me almost as much as my own and although she has left me, I cannot leave her. I need her to find my prince. I follow her. I pick her thoughts like ripe pieces of fruit, and I conceal them, hidden in my pocket. When the moment is right, I hold them to my lips and with a breath that originates so deep inside me that it makes me quiver, I send them out into the waking world. With a smell that is as acute as any shark, I cast an all seeing glance. At times I am able to pull the tubes from my body and walk the walk of a ghost, but not today. Today, she will come to me…I see her looking sad and forlorn.

There, my dreamer. I still remember that night. We are both living it. The wheel. It will not stop spinning.

The building is not the type that could ever look cheerful. There is something about the thick stone and the green vines that make it look dreary during the winters and suffocating during the summer or perhaps this is just a projection of Safia's loneliness. Safia feels a pang of guilt every time she looks at its gray, dreary walls. It is not the type of place to leave someone, especially a loved one, but that is exactly what Safia had done. This is exactly the thorn in her heart. She can still feel her presence, like a limb that's been amputated. "Are you there?" she wants to call out.

Always, I reply. I know she can hear me.

Today is a cloudy day, the type of day that threatened rain. The hospital seemed to blend into its overcast landscape. Every time Safia comes here she feels time stand still, as if she has never left. The building has its secrets. Safia is no stranger to this truth. Unconsciously, the building begins to epitomize all that Safia has sought to overcome and thus, becomes an opponent. Every time she sees the structure she tries to master it, to lay dominion over it, but the building is always too clever for her.

Safia sucked in her breath. *What a wretched day*, she thinks looking up at the sky, wondering when lightning will strike. She hates her appointments here. No matter how hard she tries to be late, she is always on time.

The first receptionist waves her through; the second signs her in. They are all nondescript women with pleasant smiles. They could be twenty, or they could be forty. The floor that Safia enters has plush carpets, fancy art, and classical music playing in the background. It is for the outpatients — to put them at ease, as if that were possible.

We're an instant gratification culture and waiting is never easy. In fact, waiting alone, armed with only one's thoughts and some old magazines can be the toughest thing in the world. It's times like this that Safia wishes her mind could wander, instead of remaining annoyingly blank—like a door that has been bolted shut. Her thoughts and memories are stored and archived, held in place by a powerful gatekeeper called dread. It's dread that prevents them from seeping in through the cracks. It's not easy to trick the gatekeeper, but it is possible. There's always a password, a magical key that will lift the charm, unlock the gate...unleash the flood. Now she is in his world.

"Relax, and let your mind go blank," her shrink says as if an empty room will fool the gatekeeper; trick him to let down his guard. There is no music in this room. He's sitting in a leather chair. As far as shrinks go he is highly qualified and extremely reputable. His demeanor is calm and collected to say the least. His words are equally soothing and should be reassuring, but they're not. Safia is only irritated by his words. She is irritated by the patience in his eyes, the timber of his voice, and the echo in the room. He had the type of voice that, if Safia weren't careful, might hypnotize her. Safia lets his words fall into nothingness.

"Relax and let your mind go blank. Focus on one feeling at a time."

But, this only makes her feel trapped, grates on her nerves. How do people focus on one feeling at a time? There is never just one. Safia has become accustomed to either emptiness or a flood. How do people pull them apart, disentangle one silk thread from the other. For a long moment there is only silence and then someone starts tapping on Safia's door. It's guilt. Yes, guilt, there's a feeling. How about loneliness? There's another one.

"Good, identifying your feelings is a start. You're making progress."

Shame is about to come in, but Safia closes the door and focuses on the "progress" that she's making.

"Do you remember anything about that night?"

That night, Safia only remembers that it was dark.

"No, I don't."

"Hmmm…okay."

He sounds condescending as if she's not doing her job, keeping up her end of the bargain. It annoys her.

"Why do you keep asking me that? If there was something important it would have been in the police report."

"I don't know, you tell me? You seem to be avoiding it. Every time we bring it up, you seem restless…edgy. "

Safia found herself suddenly wishing that the session were over. There is a loose strand on her sweater that she slowly starts picking apart, wondering how much she can unravel. She tries to go back to that night. It had been dark. They had been bickering. Something had distracted her and that's what had caused the accident.

This is as far as Safia is able to go. Even this has left an acrid taste in her mouth. It is the taste of bitterness threatening to rise up and choke her. It lay on her tongue and in her taste buds as if she had swallowed bitter chilies or sour milk. She can feel it in the guilt that lays buried in her gut or the regret that eats away at the lining of her stomach. She can smell its putrid odor with each breath, each inhale until the suffocation becomes unbearable. Safia has no choice but to run out of the building, past a room full of waiting patients, and past the receptionist and outside into the fresh air where gasping, she takes long deep breaths like a person drowning, like a person who's just come up from underwater.

Safia stands trembling and shaking in the cool autumn air. When she regains her composure, a significant amount of time has passed. She debates going back inside. It would be the right thing to do. Another five minutes pass and then an hour. With a heavy heart she turns away from the building that both beckons and repels her. I'm sorry. I've failed you, she thinks.

And although I am so close, I merely watch her leave knowing there is nothing I can do to make her stay.

Safia is in the safety of her tiny loft, the glow of the laptop screen illuminating her face; a pile of half read books on her night table; a framed photo carefully face down on her bookshelf and all around her is controlled chaos. Someone might think she was a little bit of a hoarder if they did not know any better. She had paintings, knick-knacks, and jewelry casually left on the end tables. The laptop is set up in a little nook that looks over the city. It is her refuge and her prison. Safia is not quite agoraphobic, not yet, but when the worst storms hit many months can pass by before she comes out for air.

Safia scans the headlines on her laptop. There is a story on the net about a homeless man being beaten to death by a gang of youths, thirteen and fourteen-year-old boys; a man having been accused of stealing from his company opens fire on his co-workers; an Islamophobe shoots a pregnant Muslim woman. Outside she can hear the siren of an ambulance. Everyone is on edge. There is something in the pulse of the city that isn't quite right. Safia has been feeling it for a while now lingering overhead—like a dark spell or an evil enchantment.

Safia checks her messages. There are three new creative briefs in her in-box and an urgent message on her cell phone. She decides to check the message first. At first there is nothing, dead air and then the abrupt giggle of her cousin Hinna as she announces her engagement. Her voice is all sweet and bubble gummy. Even as Safia listens to the message she can see Hinna's favorite colors. He just proposed last night and she's been on the phone all day. Most relatives would have sounded nervous, waited to tell Safia last, but not Hinna—that's what she's always liked about her. Of course, there's another reason. Hinna hates getting things off the rack: invitations, dresses, décor. She wants Safia to help design her wedding. Safia hates long elaborate weddings, but adores her cousin so the decision is pretty clear. Her mother thinks it's a great idea.

"It'll get you out of that tiny little apartment of yours. Give you a chance to meet people."

"Hmmm…," grunts Safia over the phone, not wanting to let on that she agrees. It always irritates her when she and her mother are on the same page. She makes a show of independence even though she knows her mother is right.

"It's not my place," she wants to say, but to placate her mother Safia gives in; and for once, I agree. How curious, in my absence she has inherited my friends.

She meets Hinna right away at a little café. Cousin was not known for her patience. It's the type of shop that sells fancy coffee and overpriced sandwiches. Hinna is there early. When Safia walks in, Hinna has a coffee in front of her and is nibbling on a biscotti. She gives Safia a big hug, her coppery hair hanging loosely down her shoulders like a thick roll of silk. It is only in the last couple years that they have become close. Hinna was amongst the first people to reach out to her after the accident.

The first fifteen minutes are spent going over the details of the proposal and oohing and ahhing over the ring. Safia has never been into jewelry, but this ring is a beaut. The way it sparkles, the way it catches the light. A person could get lost looking at that ring; several people turn their heads to look. I can see it now, the fairy tale wedding and even from my sleeping bed, I am jealous.

Now Safia's role comes in—of course there's a catch. Hinna wants Safia to help her plan her big day, even design the dress.

Slave labor, now that's the Hinna we know and love.

"I'm not a fashion designer. I don't know anything about clothes. I design ads for consumer products," says Safia.

"I know, but you have a great sense of color and fabric and texture. I can figure out what I want the dress to look like. I just need, you to help me with the fabric, the details, the embroidery."

"Oh, I don't know."

"You have the entire design studio at your disposal—not to mention all those little elves."

"That's not what I'm supposed to be doing at work…"

Safia is about to continue, but Hinna gives her one of her, you're really being a stick in the mud looks.

"OK fine. What's your theme?"

"I feel like… Cinderella would be appropriate."

"Umm…you're a rich princess."

"I know, but I feel like I've been swept off my feet. He's my Prince Charming."

"OK. What colors do you like?"

"I'm thinking an explosion of pink."

"Are you thinking a sari or a langha?" Safia asked, purposely using the traditional word for skirt.

"A langha...definitely!"

Safia realizes that for someone who doesn't know what she wants, Hinna has thought about her big day down to the most microscopic detail. Safia has begun to jot down notes and ideas and is mentally going over them as she walks home. It's just after dusk and the city has begun to turn as it always does. Safia has always believed that this piece of time, in between day and night is the most dangerous part of the evening. It is no man's land.

Safia is still thinking about her cousin's request for an 'explosion of pink' when she feels her spine tingle. Unconsciously, she holds her purse a little tighter, her breath becomes a little shorter, but when she looks around it's only a bum in the alley. He reeks and he's covered himself up with newspapers. Still, he's rather decrepit looking with a hunched back, bushy eyebrows and a prominent overbite. Safia is not the only one whom he makes nervous. He is awake and alert staring intently at passersby. People hurry past him, avoiding his gaze, as if this alone can make him invisible. It occurs to Safia that perhaps he's just as afraid of them as they are of him. It's what attracts and repulses her most about the city - its ability to make people vanish in plain sight.

Alan Memorial Hospital

In the morning light it is apparent that someone has been taking care of the girl in room 7A. Her hair has been combed, her nails painted, even her cheeks appear slightly rouged. People walking by always glance back careful not to wake her although this is not possible. She seems at peace, not just a shell in the way some coma patients appear.

There is something about the girl that invites people to enter, perhaps stand at her doorway for a few minutes. Many are compelled to speak to her, "Hi princess…How you doing princess?" Rather than sorrow, she seems to compel optimism in people. Perhaps, because she appears timeless, as if she will never grow old, never age. There is one person who routinely visits, but never enters her room. He stands outside her room in his white coat, and stares from the window before he finally leaves. A broken heart, no doubt.

Sarah, one of the nurses, stares at the girl for a moment. She has a full mouth, set in a way that seems like she is chewing on her thoughts, getting ready to speak her mind. Even the girl's eyes that are closed beneath their lids, seem alert as if they are looking at her. Is that even possible? Sarah wonders, can someone see through closed eyes?

Aidan has been dreaming about a girl, but that was not the problem. The problem was it was always the same girl, night after night. Every night he saw something different about her. She was always unattainable, always leading him someplace, but never letting him find her. He always woke-up just as he was about to reach out and touch her, leaving him with the feel of her soft skin on his fingertips or the fragrance of her hair. Aidan took this as a sign that he was attracted to women out of his league.

He felt like he was going through a midlife crisis of sorts. Aidan had taken to aimlessly walking and thinking about his life, and possibly where this girl fit in. With nowhere in particular to go after work he would walk to the point where he himself had begun to wonder what he was looking for. Perhaps it was randomness or some internal compass that led him to a cozy little café at the end of the street. He was surprised at how much he had been tempted to go inside, order a frothy concoction, pull out a newspaper, and watch the world go by. And then he saw Hinna in the window.

She had long hair that rippled down her back in loose waves, that perfectly made-up face, and a pair of scary stilettos that let people know she was high maintenance. She had been holding her cell in her perfectly manicured hands, a huge rock on her finger. She looked vaguely familiar reminding Aidan a little too much of his ex-fiancé. It had been enough to make Aidan cross the street. He hadn't thought twice about that decision, not until now that is, and only now because he was tired.

He was especially tired of looking at numbers. Always trying to make sense of data that has been collected from a multitude of sources. Now he employs and adjusts sophisticated algorithms, leaning back in his chair wondering how something that looks so elegant can go so wrong. Fortunately he is distracted from his self-pity by a text he's just received.

It's from Art Fishman, although no one has called him that since college. Since Aidan has known him, he's always been The Fish, or simply Fish. A fellow Harvard man, Fish is an old college pal currently working in Estate Planning for the super wealthy, a demographic that is getting smaller by the minute. Fish wants to know if he's up for drinks later that evening. Fish has an idea. In fact, Fish always has an idea and more than once Aidan has been taken in by one of his cockamamie schemes.

Still, Aidan is curious and tired of wandering the streets alone like a phantom after work. He thinks that Fish is already so bored of his chosen line of work that it's making him more off the wall than usual, which is saying a lot for Fish, but it's this intrinsic Fishness that makes Aidan like him so much. Moreover, Fish is convinced that Aidan is some kind of genius. Any day now he's going to find a way to topple the market, make a killing and Fish wants to be in on the comeback. It's ludicrous really. It's agood thing that Fish still has his day job because when it comes to anything else, he doesn't have a practical bone in his body. If he wanted a fly by night scheme, they were a dime a dozen back in the day when anyone worth an Ivy League dime was starting his own hedge fund.

The thing about Fish is that he casts his net wide and has always been good at keeping in touch with people; a couple common friends may show up, a couple of Fish's colleagues and then a couple of wildcards to keep the night interesting. Last time, Fish brought in a man from tinsel town — a director. A short man with a receding hairline who would only eat sushi, flirt wildly with the waitresses, and claim he was being haunted by his grandmother. He was good for a couple of bizarre stories about the who's who of Hollywood — shit the enquirer wouldn't even print.

Aidan has played the hermit for a little too long, and he could use a stiff drink. He dials Fish's number. His secretary puts him on hold. It may be a few minutes. Aidan stares out the window of his office. It's a great view of Manhattan, not too high, nor too low. Aidan puts down the phone and begins to rub his eyes...flakes of color seem to fall from the sky. They are the aftermath of a multi-colored tornado that sweeps across the skyline. All along the street everyone has stopped: pedestrians, shopkeepers, even motorists. They have all left their respective shelters to come outside and stare at the sky. They hold out their arms as if receiving God's bounty, but no sooner do the flakes hit the ground than they are gone.

"Hello...hello..." calls Fish from the other end of the phone.

"Hey Fish, are you near a window? There's something you gotta see."

Unfortunately, as it turned out Fish was not near a window and did not see the multi-colored phenomenon, nor did anyone else he knew. He tried to bring it up when he was having dinner at his parent's' house. It was an evening that began uncomfortably and grew progressively more unbearable. His father, a retired professor, was the classic armchair expert. Aidan, who had always gotten along well with his father, had recently developed a distaste for academics. They got on his nerves, much like back seat drivers. He didn't want to seem arrogant, but let's face it, those who can do and those who can't...well it's not something he should bring up with his father, but now and then he came pretty close. Hence, a conversation that started about the economy, which could have no good outcome, eventually led to Aidan's career. So Aidan did something much worse, he steered the conversation to the weather. If his parents thought he was turning into a crackpot before, now they would definitely wonder what he'd been smoking.

"Hey…did anyone see the abrupt change of weather this afternoon?"

"What? What are you talking about?" His mother looked up with sudden worry.

"Well…you know it became really windy and there were some flakes."

"Flakes, oh God I hope not. I still haven't brought in some of my plants."

"I hope we're not getting flurries this early. I was hoping to play a little golf over the weekend," said his father.

"No, they weren't actually those types of flakes."

"What type of flakes were they?"

"Wasn't there anything on the news…about the weather? Maybe, maybe it was just a one off thing."

By now his parents were looking at him a little quizzically.

"You know sweetheart, you're probably working a little too hard. I'm going to set the table for dinner. Samar is upstairs freshening up after her nap."

It's not that family dinners were rare in the Musawi household nor that it was odd for his Aunt Samar, who was visiting from California to join them, it was that the longer the evening progressed, the more it felt like an intervention. His parents had taken Aidan's broken engagement sadly and in due course, but now they felt it was time for him to get back on the saddle, get his life together which they felt was going nowhere. His older sister, Amina, who had done everything right including become a doctor, was there with her husband, Kevan, who had just made partner at his firm.

Amina was smart, athletic, and outgoing. It was easy to see why she had always been his father's favorite. While Aidan preferred to play by himself, did not like running around outside, and cried when his sister hit him. He could still see her now. Amina at seven years old, tall for her age and a little chubby with a close cropped boyish haircut throwing, no barreling a huge ball in his direction, hitting him in the face and knocking him down. Aidan at three was a little scrawny and slightly effeminate with big, doe eyes and dark lashes. Auntie Samar used to jest, "Looks like we know who got the looks in the family." It wasn't until college that Aidan's talents began to emerge.

Given Aidan's predicament, Auntie Samar's presence at their dinner table that night could have hardly been a coincidence. Having married off all of her own children, the old bat now spent her time arranging happy marriages for those left behind. Funny, Aidan had never thought of not having a wife as being 'left behind'. Every time he thought of her, he was reminded of that nursery rhyme; there was an old woman who lived in a shoe. She had so many children she didn't know what to do.

Still, his mother felt, and of course his aunt agreed that any man of a certain income and education that has hit his thirties without entering wedded bliss was in desperate need of a wife. The two were ready with pictures of eligible candidates spanning from North America to Europe, even bringing in his sister and brother-in-law as reinforcements—clearly everyone was interested in his marital status.

The girls in the pictures were all certainly pretty enough and smart enough—not a single ugly stepsister in the lot. It was the fact that after over thirty years of life Aidan was not sure who he was anymore—definitely not Prince Charming. It was as if there was something fundamental out there that he had failed to grasp and the path and the people and the life he had been so sure of only a year or two earlier now seemed so vapid, banal, and predictable. He had done all of this before…before the engagement, the fiancé, the fairytale castle…only to realize how little it mattered. How little he cared.

That was it, wasn't it? It had all disintegrated before him and he hadn't even cared. There was no use trying to explain this to his family. His mother would only look at it as 'I'm never going to have another grandchild'. At least Amina had dutifully already given them at least one. His father would look at him like he was shirking his responsibility, eyeing him with a stare that said, "I always knew you'd buckle, Son."

As the never ending dinner progressed and more and more food got piled onto his plate—because that's what mothers did—Aidan never looked so forward to coffee and dessert, which he gulped down with all the elegance of a hog snarfing down truffles—practically scorching his tongue and the roof of his mouth. The best thing that Aidan could do was create a diversion.

"I gotta run. I'm meeting some friends after dinner."

"At this hour?" inquired his mother.

"Mom, the city doesn't stop at 10:00 p.m."

Let his parents think that he was out partying, sowing his wild oats. "I'm still young, there's still time before I settle down. I just gotta get some stuff out of my system first."

Aidan's words sounded weak even to himself. It made Aidan glad to have Fish's invitation, glad to have somewhere to go tonight. Something to do that would help ignore that nagging feeling in the pit of his stomach, the despair so palatable that it was seductive. He had an overwhelming urge to let go…to fall in and be the instrument of his own demise. Taking a deep breath, he realized that he hadn't hit rock bottom yet—but it was there waiting for him.

It was the type of place people went to be seen. At one point it was a watering hole for cocky investment bankers, lawyers, and real estate developers who bragged about their latest deals to the beautiful women—models, gold diggers, and socialites—falling at their feet. Alas, in a volatile market that was riding high one day and low the next, it could not have fallen farther from grace, with Wall Street men who were considerably less cocky and the beautiful women becoming more aloof. There was a raggedness to the men— disheveled suits, bloodshot eyes, dark circles, and nervous twitches—as if they had not spent their day in comfortable offices, but toiling in dark, treacherous mines. It could be seen on their faces—grumpy, dreamy, bashful, stealthy, dopey, and sneezy. They might as well have been dwarves trying to forget their day in the mines, or avoid thinking about what they faced tomorrow. The women sensed this, much in the same way they can sense a man's net worth and make them work harder.

When Aidan arrived, Fish was already there with his blazer off, his tie loose, and was drinking by himself at a booth. Fish always had this underlying nervous energy about him. Although he'd never been the jumpy type, he was easily excitable. His face was flushed and his posture relaxed—all the indications that he was in a good mood. Fish waved him over and no sooner did his gaze leave Aidan, when his eyes settled on a pretty, cocktail waitress. Fish had never been married, but had been in a string of relationships— secretaries, cocktail waitresses, and receptionists.

They were like pretty goldfish. Everything was really great, until it wasn't and then Fish would start to realize that his goldfish was really a shark. Currently, Fish was sharkless, but that wouldn't be for long. Fish was a glutton for punishment.

Aidan sat down. It felt good to be in a place like this, to have his senses overpowered by the music, the noise, the women, and the drinks. Fish greeted him in the usual way, asking the usual questions. There was something comforting in the predictability of male camaraderie.

After a few drinks Aidan relaxed, his back becoming a little less straight, his shoulders a little more slumped, his stance a little less defensive. He eased into the evening by unloading about his job, his boss, the painful family dinner. He stopped short of the colorful tornado in the sky. Aidan was not that drunk. Not yet.

"Hey, I'm with you," agreed Fish. "No reason to tie yourself down to the old ball and chain. You just got free. You just gnawed off your own foot to save your life."

"I wouldn't go that far. She was the one who dumped me."

"Tomato, Tomahto"

Fish had never liked Aidan's fiancée. They grated on each other's nerves like cats and dogs. Neither understood what Aiden saw in the other.

"Anyway, there are plenty of fish in the sea, don't just sit on the sidelines dipping your toe in the shallow end. Take a plunge—maybe tonight!" said Fish eyeing a gorgeous brunette in the corner.

"Yeah, I don't know if that's going to help me. Something weird is going on…"

"What do you mean?"

Aidan was saved from continuing by the arrival of a couple more friends and, of course, the wild card. This time the guy was an inspirational speaker. He had given a presentation at Fish's firm.

Fish put his arm around his new best friend. "I'm telling you, this guy changed the way I think."

Personally, Aidan had never thought much of this new breed of voodoo doctors. He didn't believe in just thinking a life into existence. Aidan noted that the others also looked skeptical. This could be an interesting evening, thought Aidan. It would take a couple drinks, but he would enjoy picking this guy apart. But as the evening progressed, something strange happened. Aidan felt oddly disconnected from himself as if he were a third party watching the gathering—a fly on the wall. He was there, but he was not there. It left him feeling unsettled, not unlike like those nights he'd been having, when he'd wake up feeling like he'd never really slept at all...

CHAPTER SIX

In dreams I am formidable.

Slowly, I am painting a picture…drawing a map. Too long I have lain here alone. She must know this. She must see that I still need her, for she has never stopped being a part of me and in this regard, I employ a little wickedness…a little smoke, even a little fire. It has never left me. I can still feel it stinging my eyes, burning my throat and heat emanating from my body as if the fire is inside not out and in a way, it is.

It is only by my hand, my cool, inviting touch that she can be led out of this nightmare. This nightmare that she has escaped a thousand times over. I am there to hold her hand, even as she lets mine slip…even as I fall into darkness and become mist. As mist I am untouchable, unbreakable. It is the state I am when I see her flutter her pretty eyes, wash away the last remnants of the night, in a way that I cannot. I can see the slight twitch of her mouth before it breaks out into a yawn, grateful for the day ahead. Yet again, I am left behind no more tangible than a wisp of air living eternally in the shadows of that night that neither one of us can fully escape.

I see her in her little loft now tossing and turning. She is becoming a little mad. Come into my world I want to say. Let me embrace you. Let the wheel finally stop spinning. But even here she is reluctant to meet me. *No matter. I travel through the waking world like mist.* Mist imprints itself on all it touches, seeping into your pores until it is a part of your skin.

When Safia woke up that morning it was not the dream she usually had, the one that left her trembling in her sleep. Instead, it was to the sound of loud jarring discourse, voices that punctured her sleep. She had had this conversation before, many times and it always ended differently. Just when Safia was about to add her two cents she opened her eyes and floated back to her quiet little loft. Still confused for a moment, she lay there listening to the sounds of her neighborhood, a dog barking on the street, a neighbor rustling, and a door slamming. The voices lingered in the background and if she strained her ears against the sound of traffic, she could still hear them.

It was only 5 a.m., much earlier than she expected, so she hit the snooze button and went back to sleep. When she woke up again her head still felt cloudy and muddled from dozing in and out of no man's land; neither world being able to hold its claim on her. Perhaps, that's why she felt so tired. Still, Safia rolled out of bed, stretched her legs, and did what she always did first thing in the morning—checked her email while munching on a chocolate chip cookie, before heading to the bathroom to get ready for work.

There were two emails from her mother and three already from Hinna with websites and links she was meant to check out. Safia opened her mother's email. Her mother always wrote as if she had just come out of the early nineteenth century. The email began…My darling daughter… It read like a family newsletter and there was a list of relatives she was meant to get in touch with to offer either congratulatory remarks regarding births, engagements, gradations, or condolences and sympathies regarding death, disease, and other untimely events. It was her mother's way to try and draw Safia back into social life and show the community that Safia had not become some hermit locked up in a tower. Her mother's biggest fear was that people would begin to talk about her reclusiveness. Rumors would spread and that would jeopardize Safia's chance for a normal life.

Safia was looking forward to arriving at work early today, but no matter what time she left she found that the subway was always crowded, there was always someone walking too slowly on the sidewalk in front of her and there was always a line-up for coffee. It made Safia wish that she still had her car, not that it would be much use in the city.

Safia had not driven in years, not since she had been a cocky teenager. The smog and congestion of the city brought it all back to her. Her senses felt overwhelmed. She wondered if she could get behind the wheel again or even get into a cab without feeling anxious. Just thinking about it made her smell smoke. Safia could remember clearly the smell of smoke…

There was so much smoke it made her eyes burn. She would blink her eyes over and over again, hoping to clear the haze; her hands clutched the wheel with all her strength. If she could just hang on and of course, the loud jarring voices. Voices that at one time had thought they were invincible.

She was driving fast, faster than she should have been for that time of night. It should have been like any other night, but she felt something go wrong. A twist of fate, a bump in the road, a prick of a needle. All of sudden the wheel had taken on a mind of its own, twisting this way and turning that way as if possessed. Safia struggled with all her might to keep control of the wheel...so many bumps in the road— trees and bushes flying past, shadows taunting them from every corner. It was like being on a haunted roller coaster, and then like all nightmares, it ended with a scream.

When Safia arrived at work she found a group of her colleagues huddled around the computer. Orchid was laughing her deep throaty laugh, the one that came straight from the gut and Neal towered behind her with a wide grin. Safia had arrived just as the video was being played yet again. What started out as a story in a local paper had ended up a parody on late night TV and was now all over social media. Safia recognized the caricatures of the suburban youth and the homeless man. Safia had thought the video was in bad taste and exploited the worst possible aspects of human nature. She cringed the first time she saw it, but now with Neal and Orchid's commentary it brought a smile to her face. They had further morphed the video into something that was uniquely theirs...only in the Dream House. Taking it one step further, Neal had the idea of modifying the concept for a client's print ad.

The client, a soft drink company, hugely popular among young adults and teens was looking for something a little edgy. The beverage came in an assortment of eccentric flavors that few self-respecting adults would be caught dead chugging, flavors like Vomit, Boston Cream, Philly Cheese Steak, and Morning Bacon.

Safia wondered what the appeal was in drinking a vomit flavored beverage. She wondered what her parents would think if they saw her drinking Vomit—probably that she needed to increase her sessions with the head shrink. Mucus, a brand new flavor would be coming out shortly.

It was no wonder that Neal could think of such a fitting ad. It was the type of beverage that people in the Dream House might be seen drinking. Flavors that could have been dreamed up in someone's colorful dystopia. In Hell, there is fire and brimstone and Mucus flavored soda; the type of world where opposites are the norm, where dreams are nightmares and nightmares are dreams. Where what is normally considered revolting is now considered refreshing. Have some mucus flavored soda with a maggot burger and a side of freshly fried earthworms. Perhaps emotions could also be turned into beverages...hope, love, despair. What would be in a beverage called despair?

Safia imagined it would be a very thick ice cream shake, flavored like dark licorice, the taste would be horrible, but it would have enough caramel in it to make people take another gulp. They would know that it was bad for them, but they would keep coming back. It would stick to their throats as they swallowed, coating their esophagus with ooze making them want to choke, but they wouldn't be able to stop drinking, they would drink and drink and drink until they'd vomit…that was how despair worked.

Safia had four new creative briefs waiting for her when she reached her desk. Now, more and more of her briefs contained conceptual rather than technical guidelines, letting her play around with ideas and themes, implementing the type of vision that was generally expected from an Art Director. It was a good thing. It should have been a good thing, but it made Safia nervous. She could feel the hairs on her back stand on end as she read the description. It wasn't that she couldn't do it…she could. Playing around with concepts and ideas meant letting the mind wander and there was no telling what associations it would make. It was the type of activity she hated in therapy, but somehow it worked really well for her job. All those cobwebs and dark corners, never knowing what was lurking behind them. Sometimes she suspected that she was being watched. Someone was watching her from inside herself. She could feel it in the corners of her mind. Sometimes she would even catch a glimpse just before she fell asleep, of something so delicate it barely had any substance at all.

Many of the creatives in the Dream House also looked a little haunted, like they had an inner demon or two that they had nailed shut in their mental closet. These monsters were the same sneaky assed monsters that would hide under children's beds, waiting for when they were most vulnerable before coming for them, usually when they were just about to fall asleep. Demons always had to be fed; they were carnivorous, hungry always wanting sacrifices, always needing to be appeased.

Sometimes people were so haunted that they eventually became the demon that haunted themselves, thought Safia as she glanced over at Neal. He was leaning perilously back in his chair as if he had learned to defy gravity, eyes bloodshot, coffee in hand and his long legs draped over his desk unconcerned by his precarious state. Other worldly didn't begin to describe him; vampiric didn't begin to describe him. Neal's demon was always crawling out of its cage and whenever they all went out together Safia could never be sure who was talking. She never saw him drink, never saw him snort, never saw him inhale, he was never out of sight for a second, yet there was some pretty twisted voices coming out of his head. It made Safia want to ask, "Who am I talking to now?"

Safia had seen this demon once. Others may have disregarded the entire incident, but Safia saw it for what it was. It had happened just before the long weekend. It had been an exhausting week but no one was near packing up, even those that had turned in their assignments still lingered around. The studio could be a really chill place to hang out for those that didn't have to work. By 8:00 p.m. anyone who was still there ended up at the bar downstairs where people from the surrounding firms congregated, and where the creatives from the Dream House always stood out. Unlike the suits that always blended together, this group was as diverse as it came. There was the Queen type, the Goth type, the Apple Pie American, and everything in between. Safia could feel heads turn as they walked in through the door and started to settle in and then take over the bar, no one could say they were a quiet bunch.

She hadn't wanted to stay late, but once the lobster macaroni and truffle fries arrived Safia remembered how famished she was — food in mouth, drink in hand, Safia had to admit that this was the most amusing lot she had ever met. Although the neighboring suits looked at them as if they were a bunch of social deviants, they were responsible for some of the most ingenious ad campaigns today. With few inhibitions, this group was more entertaining than an episode of "Saturday Night Live." It was like being part of a circus and perhaps that's why Safia didn't notice that it kept getting later and later.

I should go home, Safia kept thinking but then someone would stop her…five more minutes, and then five more and before Safia knew it, the street had turned into a very different street, the bar a very different bar. Gone were the suits that came in for a drink after work, this was just their first stop anyway. It should have been a clue, but it wasn't…

Had Safia not walked out without her purse, she would have missed it. Had she not had to turn back the moment she hit the exit sign, she would have been halfway down the block towards the subway or she would have been hailing a cab using one of the taxi chits she had left in her wallet. If Safia had been paying attention, she would have noticed this guy eyeing them for the last hour. He and his friends had been sitting at a small table in the corner. He could have been a suit having a bad day, he could have been a regular working class schmo that walked into the wrong bar. He looked at them like they were escapees from the local asylum.

Safia remembered she could see him walking towards her as she came back inside. It looked like he was heading for the door until someone stepped in front of him blocking his path, eclipsing her view. By this time Safia had come close enough to hear him mutter something like, "bunch of freaks…"

She didn't know if he was pissed at Lorenzo specifically, a neurotic chain smoking little man. Perhaps if this guy had been less drunk, perhaps if Lorenzo hadn't been so frail, he might not have tried to bulldoze his way past him, but Safia heard someone say, "Hey, what did you say…?"

It was Neal. Ice, was the only way to describe it, cold blue ice in the sound of his voice. When she looked up, he was standing there looking seven feet tall, skin luminescent, eyes blazing endless pools of darkness…a dark angel. All of a sudden everything went quiet as if everyone in the bar was holding their breath. Safia could hear a hissing sound in her ear, a soft buzzing. It wasn't that Neal was a masochist or a sociopath, but he could be. At that moment he looked like a Vampire swooping down for the kill, and then someone put a hand on Neal's shoulder and his face softened. He let out a roaring laugh that was part amusement and part threat and then it was over, the party resumed.

Alan Memorial Hospital

It is the middle of the night at the hospital. Sarah is at the nurse's station by herself. Maria is running late. It doesn't matter; this time of night is always quiet. When Maria gets there she's out of breath and in a frenzy. Sarah can't wait to hear what happened this time, but she sees a patient's light is on. This will only take a second, she thinks.

The lights have been dimmed; the hallways are empty. She can hear people sleeping softly, now and then letting out soft moans. When she gets to the room the woman is fast asleep. Sarah straightens out her covers and looks at her chart. On her way back she passes room 7A. Rarely has she been here at night, but something catches her eye...a flicker of light on the monitor, something that might almost pass as brain activity, must be a trick of the eye...an anomaly.

Sarah steps inside. The patient is sleeping peacefully. Such a young girl, the staff has nicknamed her Sleeping Beauty. It may be her vulnerability or the fact the she looks so helpless, but Sarah is compelled to hold her hand. She is about to leave when she feels something, a tremor. This is highly unusual, amazing even. She'll have to let the doctors know in the morning.

～

It was enough to make Aidan choke, but Fish just sat there grinning like he had just unveiled the friggin' Mona Lisa, as Aidan went down in a coughing fit. Aidan felt his throat constrict; the air passage tighten, the shrimp become larger. As the jumbo shrimp obstructed his breathing, Aidan could feel his hands go to his throat and that's when the sensation hit him. It was the sensation of floating outside his body. Is this what dying felt like? And he began to panic. He felt himself gasp for air and just before he was about to lose it, he felt something...another sensation.

Like a warm wave passing through him, not unlike an embrace. There is a fragrance too, a scent that has become all too familiar. Aidan begins to relax. He is not going to die today. Fish, a little slow on the ball, finally came to his senses and vehemently started slapping him on the back, before reaching around and implementing the Heimlich maneuver. All it took was one strong thrust to dislodge the crustacean and send it flying across the room. The shrimp having finally become airborne sped out like a missile until it lost velocity and plopped down into a fruity cocktail and sank to the bottom. The owner engaged in an animated conversation remained blissfully unaware of the disturbance to his drink...serves him right, for ordering an Appletini!

"Are you alright, pal?" asks Fish.

"Yeah," says Aidan clearing his throat and taking a sip of water. He looks around the room, his eyes lingering in the dark corners. It wasn't even close to last call, yet the lounge was almost empty. Fish's voodoo doctor had been spouting his gospel all night as if they were his flock. Aidan didn't know whether to laugh or punch him in the face.

Jack Westland was one of those guys that Aidan hated almost instantaneously. For one thing he was too good looking. His plucked eyebrows, his highlighted hair, his manicured fingernails, along with his too suave voice wreaked of failed actor. Jack Westland always spoke as if there was a camera pointing right at him. Guys like that ought to be shot, thought Aidan, that's why when Fish first suggested it, he thought it was a joke.

"As soon as I saw this guy I thought of you," said Fish

"Ummm...sure."

"Who else but you would appreciate what an amazing opportunity this is?"

An amazing opportunity for what? To become officially brain dead? There's no way I'm signing up for this lunatic's program, thought Aidan. If Fish even suggested it he'd get up and leave. If he wanted to throw away his money he'd put it into a hedge fund.

"This is a great opportunity. This guy, this guy here is a goldmine. I'm talking books, CDs, retreats, talk show appearances. You should have seen him in action today. He owned that stage. 'Your life in motion' isn't that brilliant? Everyone came out of that seminar feeling like they owned the world. I was in tears and that's when I thought what a spectacular investment! Let's bring this type of affirmation to everyone and I talked Jack here, into coming out for a drink with us. I knew right away that you'd be the guy."

"The guy for what...?"

"The guy to make it all happen," said Fish as Aidan had been nibbling on a shrimp cocktail and that's when Aidan began to choke...

Now with his throat finally clear Aidan began taking deep breaths. This wasn't the first batty investment idea Fish had come to him with. Last year Fish had gotten hooked on time-share properties, owning part of a condo in Vegas and trading it for other destinations around the world. He had even gotten Aidan to sit in on a four-hour presentation. It was totally not worth the mediocre seats to Phantom of the Opera, and before that it was a shaky hedge fund and before that it was a stupid blanket with arms. Ok maybe that one wasn't so stupid!

Lord knows that Fish was rich enough but money seemed to flow out of his hands like water. Part of it was his addiction to expensive girlfriends and part of it was his attraction to off the wall investment schemes. The more mind-boggling a business proposition, the more Fish couldn't resist plunking down cash. The only thing that didn't surprise Aidan was that he hadn't come up with a scheme for spinning straw into gold. Fish, however, referred to these schemes as innovative.

Fortunately, Fish had a different persona at work with his dark suit, understated watch and the sober demeanor that was part counselor and part undertaker. It was very appropriate for handling the millions that belonged to some of their top clients. It worked well for him and Fish was one of the most popular lawyers at his firm. Fittingly, the partners in his firm weren't exactly aware of his extracurricular interests.

Fish was now looking at him with that eager, expectant look on his face like a dog waiting for his treat, while Jack looked at him with a smug expression that was half smile, half smirk of a wolf just before it sinks his teeth into someone's flesh. Aidan wanted to give him a good hard bitch slap. Time seemed to stand still, again that feeling of stepping outside oneself—like a fly on the wall—he had a bird's eye view of the entire restaurant.

He could see himself sitting there with a blotchy face, tired eyes and an expression of resignation that seem to say he's seen better days. God is that what I really look like? No wonder I can't get a date. Directly across from him Fish is twitching under the table, as if suddenly realizing that his Mona Lisa is a fake. He's tapping his fingers on his chair, a nervous gesture that's characteristically Fish and only a handful of people know about. Jack is leaning back with his shirt sleeves rolled to his elbow, his arms spread out and his shirt open halfway down to his navel. He's looking over at a drunk blonde at the next table. He's leering like an animal in front of a meat shop.

The crowd in the joint is starting to thin out. Not much to celebrate these days. A couple of tables over, the pink shrimp floats around in a colorful concoction that looks almost radioactive. Aidan and the shrimp make eye contact. The shrimp seems to read his thoughts. We're both fucked, it seemed to say. Aidan agrees. Eventually they will both be found out, and then it'll be down the toilet, but for now all either one of them can do is swim around in these highly toxic waters.

The whole experience is no more than a couple seconds and Aidan is back in his body again. All of a sudden he can feel the ground beneath his feet and a tidal wave of sound rushing through his ears. Fish and Jack are blissfully unaware that time has stopped.

"Yeah Man, it seems like an interesting proposal, but I don't know if I'm your guy."

"Look, just take a couple days and think it over."

"I don't know if a couple days are going to make a difference. I'm a numbers guy. I don't know anything about this industry. Hell, I don't even believe in this stuff. Give me an algorithm for predicting the market and I can tell you if I think it will work, but this…"

"Hey Aidan, it's not as complicated as you think. You know how to sell a good idea. You've been doing it for most of your career. With a little seed money and a little PR we can take this idea to the moon. You don't have to answer right away. Just think about it. Sleep on it for a couple days. Let's have a drink on it. Waitress, another round over here."

Fish held his glass in the air. "To new ideas and great adventures."

The three clinked glasses and as Aidan gulped down his drink, he felt that something was wrong. His drink tasted strangely bitter. It reminded him of the acrid taste of all the pungent food he had ever had. When Aidan looked up Jack and Fish's face were contorted in disgust as if they too had swallowed sour milk or bitter chilies.

The next morning Aidan had to wonder if that night had really happened. Had it not been for the horrible taste in his mouth he would have chalked it up to a bad dream, but his splitting headache indicated otherwise. He made a mental note never to go drinking with Fish again. It was past noon when his head started to clear and he started to get his appetite back and that's saying a lot in a place where half his colleagues were popping antacids. Every day there was someone either quitting or getting fired. Most of the time he didn't stand out, most of the time he was just one of the guys, but he found that some of the new execs coming on board were looking at him quizzically, like a riddle that needed to be solved. They wanted his number. It made Aidan laugh out loud to think there might be some mystery to a schmuck like him.

Aidan began reviewing the agenda for tomorrow's meeting; his secretary had just dropped it on his desk an hour ago. It had gotten to the point where they were sharing secretaries now, all part of Management's policy to trim administrative costs. Now instead of his own assistant, there was one secretary for every two executives. It was worse for those who were only lowly managers. Only the real big wigs got their own personal assistants. Aidan had asked for this agenda two days ago. As he sat reviewing the document there was a sharp knock at the door, followed by Jerry Eackland poking his head inside.

Eackland was one of the VPs at the firm. Aidan was part of his group. Jerry couldn't manage his department for shit, but he was a nice guy. As Jerry stepped inside, Aidan couldn't help but notice his belly bulging out of his pants. Everyone knew that he was going through a pretty ugly divorce; in fact his wife's family had a stake in the company so he was lucky to have this job, but it had taken a toll on him. Over the last two years Jerry had gained over twenty pounds, his eyes were bloodshot and Aidan suspected that he'd been sleeping in his office a couple nights a week.

"Aidan, how've you been doing, ready to meet with the shareholders? You know I've been looking over your numbers. You're starting to make a comeback…" and then a little more nervously, "I need you to make a comeback. The department has been counting on guys like you."

The truth was that the market these days was a crap shoot. The best way to stay safe was to stay a little bit ahead, make a little bit more on the up and lose a little less on the down. No one had expectations of being up when the market was plunging, but on the other hand, losing too much caused people to get fired.

"We're holding up Jerry."

"Up late last night?"

"Sure, kinda, you know how it is."

There was an awkward silence. Aidan got the impression that Jerry wanted to say more, but wasn't getting his opening. Aidan figured that the reminder wasn't the main reason that Jerry had paid him a visit. Part of it was to gauge how he was doing, part of it was to see if Aidan was getting ready to flee the coop and part of it was to become buds. Aidan was long past needing a mentor, but Jerry's loneliness seemed to ooze out of him like pus, from his tired eyes, to his sad receding hairline. When he lost his wife, he lost most of his friends too. Jerry was okay enough at the office, but when he wasn't talking shop he was as boring as hell. Aidan would no sooner invite out his grandmother. Aidan wasn't the only one that felt that way. Jerry was a loner. He could tell that Jerry was the kid that never made the in-crowd, was the last to be selected for every team. Still he seemed to be vying for an invitation; finally Aidan threw him a bone.

"You should come out with us sometime…"

"No kidding, that sounds great. A bunch of single guys out on the town, bet you're a real hell raiser, bet you gotta bunch of stories."

Now Jerry was doing the annoying nudge, nudge…wink, wink. Aidan was starting to regret this already. No doubt he was going to get a bunch of follow-up emails and texts from

Jerry about 'guy's night out' as if it was something they practiced religiously. In reality it was a more ad hoc system with whoever didn't have plans that night. Some days this number was significant, other times it was just Aidan and the janitor. Okay, the janitor was cleaning his office when Aidan offered him a drink, so technically it wouldn't count as drinking alone.

"Actually, Jerry we just watch sports and drink beer. Well, except for the guys in AA. They usually have flavored seltzer."

"Beer and ribs, I love it. Grub for real men."

"Yeah...umm...not everybody eats pork and a lot of the guys are watching their cholesterol so usually just go for nature burgers and Indian, sometimes sushi.

"Can't wait Bro," said Jerry as he did the old fake gun with his fingers and headed out the door. Aidan really hoped that he wasn't going to start calling him his main man. This could really get embarrassing.

Aidan hated taking cabs, but he did not bring his car to work today, his head hurt too much and he didn't want to deal with New York traffic. Still, ever since that Muslim cab driver was shot by one of his passengers he felt uneasy getting into a closed confined space with a stranger. He could see it now, with his dark hair and olive complexion he was sure to get the, "So what part of the world are you from, my friend?" And then the cabbie pulls out a gun. Some lunatic who thinks he's standing up for 9/11.

When Aidan did get a cab, the driver was a Haitian guy that did not feel like talking. Hopefully the Wall Street threads put him at ease, although now and then Aidan still got mistaken for a waiter.

As Aidan stepped into his dark apartment—one of the few luxuries he had decided to keep—and looked out onto the view of Manhattan; Jerry and Fish and even the meeting, which happened to be as pointless and confusing as a group of people sharing the same delusion, were the last thing on his mind. Right now Aidan relished being alone, even climbing into bed alone.

As he flipped through the local news he stopped at a particularly disturbing piece about a homeless man being beaten to death by a gang of local youths. A security camera had picked up the footage. The footage showed young, white fourteen-year-old boys picking on a defenseless man with a baseball bat. Looking at the footage he had to wonder did he want to be the guy with the bat or the guy taking a beating. In any case these kids were cold-blooded sharks. They may have a career on Wall Street. Then Aidan closed his eyes, once again to be led into her sweet embrace.

CHAPTER SEVEN

I drink in lost souls.

They call out to me, and it is the smell of their hunger that has brought me to this gathering. There are so many here to choose from. Like a shark, I have found my way to a school of fish. I look out into the auditorium; a sea of people look back at me. Their breaths are as sweet as honey and their desperation as rich as wine. They are mine for the taking. I pluck them from their sleep, dew still in their eyes.

It is how I like them best. How fragrant their breath, how strong their beating heart...how luscious their secrets. I have them within my grasp. It gives me courage and it keeps me alive, with their blood running strong I am not only able to fly, but also able to reach destinations I never have before. One by one, I take them in and cast them out, but there is one that I am hesitant to let go. What is it that makes me stop?

Not his mouth that is turned up in a petulant little pout...such anger, but anger is not always such a bad thing. I come a little closer. Soft lips, and silky curls, thick hair that was meant to be wrapped around one's fingers and eyes that are filled with grey.

What is it that makes my blood run cold and my heart beat faster? Can he sense me; can he feel my silvery fingers, my intent beckoning him towards me.

I must have him.

It was like watching a magician pull a rabbit out of a hat, although Aidan didn't believe in magic. He didn't believe what he was seeing right before his eyes. Aidan stood with a grimace on his face, in an auditorium full of people wondering how he got there, or more accurately how Fish had suckered him into coming. There were about fifty others sitting in the plush seats looking up at a guy that was part motivational speaker, part guru, and all wizard, and Aidan wasn't buying it.

For one thing he looked too young to really know what he was talking about. Anyone that figures out the meaning of life before forty is either a saint or a scam artist. Aidan had never bought into the think your way to a better life, he had never tried to clear his head, meditate, and smile from his liver or from his kidneys or from wherever this guy was saying, but this type of salvation was all the rage.

Maybe if this guy hadn't looked like he had just walked off the set of a soap opera. Maybe if he'd looked like he was Gandhi's twin. Maybe if he was two hundred years old instead of thirty five, and had spent the last fifty years meditating on top of a mountain, communing with nature, wearing nothing but a sarong, and eating only one meal a day of vegetables and rice. Maybe then Aidan wouldn't be sitting there looking at his tag, wondering why this idiot on stage was wearing a nicer watch than he was.

It made Aidan want to laugh or puke, or better yet, puke on Fish for dragging him here when he could be at home eating greasy take-out while reading the Financial Times, dodging phone calls from his parents, and preparing for the next impending disaster.

Despite himself, Aidan cracked a smile; Jack was now asking the audience if they were dissatisfied with their life…who the hell wasn't? Anyone could just look at the unemployment rate, and see the disparity between the rich and poor, an economy in shambles. The average Joe worked hard and was going nowhere. The not-so-average-Joe, who thought he was ahead of the game, guys who Aidan worked with every day, were running the wrong way up an escalator.

Most of his friends were either single and miserable, or married and miserable, but the most pathetic were those who were miserable, but believed they were happy. Truth was that if people were depressed about their lives, there was probably a good reason.

Now comes the, I was once in your shoes spiel. It was always the same—I came from a dysfunctional family…I was abused as a child…I was an addict. Where were all the people from a normal family, had a great relationship with their parents, grew up in the suburbs and were all round nice guys? How come they never got into this racket?

This guy's motto was all about getting what you want from the universe. The way Aidan saw it; the universe didn't owe us a thing, if anything we owed the universe. Aidan didn't believe in much, but he did believe in Karma. Aidan wasn't sure what type of Karma had brought him here today, some past misdeed or a blessing disguised as opportunity, but then the only thing more unbelievable than this guy was Fish.

Fish stood beside him mesmerized…in complete awe. He had the same goofy, dumb love expression on his face every time he met another floozy. The type of expression that meant he was going to put on a blindfold and hold out his wallet and just for good measure put his head up his ass. Only this time it was no floozy, it was Jack Westland. Although saying Jack Westland was no floozy was just a matter of semantics. The way Aidan saw it, Jack was an attention junkie, the type of guy who would sell his soul—which Aidan wasn't entirely sure he had—for a shot at the limelight. Aidan was willing to bet money that the guy had a string of failed acting…modeling…reality show attempts before settling on this venue. When the question and answer started, Aidan wanted to raise his hand and ask if he had ever been in theatre.

"What's this guy's background?" Aidan had asked Fish.

But Jack had never been an actor. According to Fish, Jack started out in the Peace Corp before a stint in India led him to leave the organization and spend a year in an Ashram. He then came back to the States to pursue a degree in journalism and work as a freelance journalist. It was all right there in the bio Aidan was holding, but the only thing Aidan could focus on was whether this guy was wearing make-up.

Oddly, Fish wasn't the only one who looked like they were eating it up. All around him people seemed fixated. The last thing Aidan wanted to do was to advocate the type of crap this guy spewed. The seminar should not have been going so well. Jack should have been laughed off the stage by now but instead, when the session ended he was reeling them in like the Pied Piper. There was a line-up of people—entranced by his music, getting autographed copies of his self-published book, "The Secret to the Universe; The Secret to You" and requesting more seminars. When Aidan saw Fish waiting for him at the end of the seminar, dispersing the crowd and handing out pamphlets to Jack's next appearance all he could think of to say was, "I guess we're in the self-help business."

"I guess we're in the self-help business…," it sounded just as lame coming out of his mouth now, as it did when he practiced it in his head. His family had never seen him as the boy genius that Wall Street did and this sounded farfetched even to him. It bore a little too much resemblance to his old college escapades; the ones he used to think were so clever.

Aidan held back on giving his family the big news as long as he could. He could see them giving him the proverbial eye roll along with the skeptical…hmmm. However, it had been so long since he had anything new to report that when they asked him what he was up to—angling for some information on his personal life— he went ahead and told them about Fish and the whole Jack Westland deal. It seemed a safer bet than bringing up his non-existent love life. Usually he was never so candid, but deep into his mother's cooking, chewing on a chicken biryani and potato samosas, while chugging mango nectar—it had been his favorite drink as a kid—he let his guard down.

The announcement was surprisingly anticlimactic. Barely an eyebrow was raised as his mother asked him if he wanted vanilla ice cream with mango sauce for dessert—another childhood favorite—or some Indian mehtai (sweets) that she had picked up from the Desi (Indian) grocery store. Aidan wondered why he couldn't just have both.

"Of course, you can have both, but you hate store bought mehtai," said his mother. "And aren't you trying to get in shape?"

"Why would I want to get in shape? I mean I am in shape," said Aidan sucking in his gut a bit. "Why is this a concern now?"

"That's good jannu. I'm not concerned, but there's going to be so many social events going on this summer and it wouldn't hurt you to look your best."

"I'm not a girl. I don't need to look my best."

"OK, then just stick with your self-help..."

"I don't need self-help. This is just a crazy business venture that Fish got me into."

"Why so defensive? I think it's wonderful that you're exploring a little self-improvement."

"Maybe it can help you get your life back on track," added his father.

"I'm not one of this guy's weirdo disciples. I'm just trying to sell his book; although it's great that you think my life needs help. Not every guru is authentic Mom, not every screwed-up life can be fixed."

"Your life's not screwed-up, just stagnating a little. You've been in a rut for a while; you've been alone for a while. I know you think you're young and you are, but life passes quickly and I want to see you happy before I die. Maybe it wouldn't hurt to give this guy a try."

"I'm fine. I'm not stagnating. I'm just doing what I always do. I'm just trying to make a living, make up for the millions that went down the crapper. Apparently a lot of people buy into this, you gotta be in tune with the universe, crap."

"There's more to life than money, and you do have to be in tune with the universe. You know I'm always right," she said raising an eyebrow.

Aidan yawned and closed his laptop. His responses to the last couple emails were already hazy in his mind. It wasn't off the wall for Aidan's parents to think he needed a little self-help. His mother was a get back on the horse kind of a woman. Aidan thought back to the events of the last couple months, truth was that there was something weird going on. It was not something he'd care to admit to his parents, let alone Fish. He could barely admit it to himself.

It was this sort of denial that kept him awake at night, which is why Aidan couldn't bring himself to go to sleep even though it was past 2 a.m. At some point the insomnia was beaten down and Aidan drifted off in his bed, but his dreams had become restless. It was because of her...

...She began leading him down a dark, tumultuous path. He did not know where they were going, but he had no choice but to follow. Then he began to smell smoke. At first it was faint, but it quickly became stronger and pungent. It was the type of smoke that lingers, the way incense lingers long after it's been burned; except this was not the sweet smell of incense. This was the type of smoke that made him want to choke, it was the type of smoke that made him think every breath was going to be his last. Before Aidan knew it, he was coughing.

Abruptly, he woke-up sure that his apartment was on fire. It was a rude awakening after a horrific dream. He had dreamed that he was barreling down a dark road. He could hear yelling and screaming, and when he woke up his eyes stung and began to water. He sat in bed quietly surveying his surroundings and then he went to the kitchen and got a couple of sleeping pills and an ice cold glass of water. It felt like heaven going down. He went back to bed, but before he fell asleep again he gasped a couple times — taking deep, deep breaths and then the smell of her perfume lulled him back to sleep.

Alan Memorial Hospital

Sarah sees the old woman sitting beside the girl's bedside. She is wearing a shawl around her head and reading something, whispering a prayer of some sort. In her hand is a small book...perhaps scripture. Her hands seem to shake some as she reaches out to the girl before her. So many times Sarah has felt the urge to reach out and smooth one of the soft tresses from the girl's forehead, just as the old woman is doing now. It is hard not to feel attached to her, to find thoughts of her nagging at the back of one's mind—following you home.

Sarah remembers the tremor she felt as she held her hand. A little wave of warmth seemed to pass through her almost felt like a subtle, electrical jolt. She debates telling the old woman about the tremor in the girl's hand, but there is something about the deeply etched lines on her face, the almost translucent wisps of hair and the hollowness in her eyes that makes Sarah decide against it. She's not even sure if the woman speaks English.

She reported the tremor to the doctor but there was no change in her condition, no indication that this was the result of some improvement. She can't help but wonder, perhaps we just need to watch a little more closely; perhaps something else will come up. Sarah sees that a patient has a call light on. She makes her way to the other end of the floor. She takes one last look back at room 7A. The girl looks serene when she is with the old woman as if she is comforted by her presence and her words.

There are times when I just watch her. I watch her alone in her apartment, hair loose and chewing on a pencil like she always did when she needed to concentrate. I notice the flecks of gold in her eyes, the way she licks her lips when she's nervous and how she pushes her hair behind her ear when she is contemplates a decision. I should have noticed before, but I didn't. There is a haunted look in her eyes that wasn't there before.

She wears her hair shorter now, while mine has grown like a vine. She has become even more of a recluse and she talks to herself. She talks to herself like a crazy person, but it is I who responds. I've never stopped talking to her…and I have never stopped waiting for her.

I watch and I wonder and I wait…but she never comes, not since the first time when we were brought here together.

But she's here now — not with me, but close by. I feel her presence. I taste her fears and she tastes mine. It is the reason why she hates it here and perhaps why she hates me, but hate is a word she doesn't know. She is biting her lips right now, which means she is extremely anxious and I am right beside her. I am so close that I can smell her breath. It smells like warm bread, like sweet raspberries, like fresh air and I want to inhale, to breathe it all in, like someone drowning. I gasp for air and once I start I cannot stop. I take in the past, all the years we've spent together. I take in the present, the hideous loneliness that binds us and I am about to take in the future, when I feel her ripped away from me. She pulls herself away and looks like she is aghast, as if she has seen something frightful.

Now she is running…and I can't stop her.

CHAPTER EIGHT

Sleep can be the best of friends or the worst of enemies. No one knows this better than Safia. No one has lived this better than Safia. Safia is awake but wishes she were asleep. It is a strange sensation, being up for this many days, but it is not the first time. There have been others. There have been nights where she lay awake staring at the ceiling, nights where she lay with her eyes closed looking into the darkness thinking that if only she could clear her head and shut off her brain sleep would come, but it never does.

There are short bursts of it throughout the night but no more as if Safia has been banned from entering this secret world, as if just as she approaches the gate she is sent back; turned away. It is the type of thing that can slowly drive a person insane, as if there isn't enough driving Safia insane, including the person sitting in front of her.

She wonders what type of game he is playing with his face serene, voice calm. Interested but detached, as if he already knows the answers but doesn't want to let on. With her head filled with smoke and her body full of lead Safia can barely think. If only she could close her eyes, it would feel so good…but the voice will not stop. There he goes again…

Safia is so tired that it is difficult to speak. There comes a point where drinking coffee just makes it worse and Safia has long given up on this measure. The entire office is getting on her nerves; hurting her eyes. It's like the sunlight is mocking her. Instead, Safia just wants to sit in a dark quiet place, where the doorway she needs might open, where she may be welcomed back to the world of sleep.

"Safia," he says gently, but with a little impatience.

"Hmmm…."

"Safia, you said you had insomnia…? Do you know what the reason is…for your insomnia?"

"I'm not sure. I guess that's why I'm here."

It's not that Safia is trying to be uncooperative; it's just that she's never understood what the point was of seeing a shrink if you had to answer your own questions.

"Survivor's guilt can be a terrible thing," he says.

"Is that what I'm feeling?"

"Do you remember when the insomnia started…start from the beginning?"

"It was the end of last week. The day we went shopping at The Annex."

"Whose idea was it to go shopping?"

"It was Hinna. She wanted to look at fabric."

"Hinna wanted to look at fabric…did Hinna know what day it was?"

"Yes…it was a Saturday. It was a Saturday morning. I met Hinna at the subway and we rode the train. The train tunnels are like a complex maze of veins and capillaries running beneath the surface of the body and we were traveling from one part of the body to another…a place deep within the mind. The three of us were an odd combination, as if the characters of a fairy tale decided to take a break and go on an excursion. Hinna was wearing a flowing skirt and walking around like a princess with her long loose hair, which made Orchid looked positively elfin, with her petite stature and spiky do…she may as well as had a pouch of pixie dust."

"And what about you Safia… What character are you?"

"I am Rapunzel."

"Ahhh…the girl stuck in the tower, so what happened when you all went shopping?"

"Nothing at first…Hinna was salivating at the mouth, as if I had taken her to a new planet. She asked 'How come you never told me about this place before?' But these were Orchid's stomping grounds. I rarely came here. It was too easy to get lost."

"Go on Safia," he said leaning in, taking his glasses off, rubbing his eyes.

Orchid knew the Annex the way a foot knows an old shoe. It was more than a market for her; it was more than a neighborhood, it was where heart lived. The Annex had long seeped into her skin and she carried it with her like an old scar. When Safia saw Orchid amidst this labyrinth, she instantly understood how a place like this could draw a person in. It was an underground market, a city within a city. The Annex was the type of place that brought a tingle up your spine.

It had everything from old medicine to modern gadgets. The first layer of merchandise was the stuff on display. This was for tourists. The best stuff was kept in the back. Orchid knew this.

Regulars often picked up purchases at the counter, few words were exchanged. In contrast, the vendors spent a lot more time talking up the newbies—probably probing to see if they were plain clothed cops—or ignored them all together. Everything was temporary here. Vendors would come, set up shop for a couple months and then they were gone, and someone new would take their place. Never had Hinna's upscale background and rose colored glasses been more apparent, as she commented on the curious smells of incense or asked vendors where they got such authentic looking items. Fortunately, they were only looking at fabric.

When Safia looked at fabric she got lost, the way someone gets lost in a good book or a fine meal. She'd look closely at the material, felt it in her hand, and held it up to the light. It was strange. Safia was not the type of person who liked to sew or had any reason for working with material, that interest always belonged to someone else. Safia would collect swatches and pair it with jewelry, antiquey looking pieces. Often desi clothing had jewels woven into the fabric and Hinna's gown would not look complete without such detail. Hinna and Orchid would look at her choices and say, "that'll never work."

"Trust me," she would say. Safia was in the zone. In her world, where she was an expert at adding depth and detail, the outcome would become an intricate labyrinth. It was how Safia often created her world…one layer at a time.

As Safia roamed deeper into the Annex, she realized that she had begun to lose sight of her friends. Orchid had run into someone she knew and Hinna had become absorbed in some vintage pieces a couple stalls down. Ordinarily, Safia did not like to wander. Wandering was dangerous; she'd lose the security of a known path—that is why it was so easy to lead her.

Quaint little antique stores are a dime a dozen—until the right one was found. When Safia wandered in, there was nothing that impressed her. They had all the same pieces she saw everywhere else — furniture from the orient, toys, art, and jewelry. Safia decided she would do a quick walk through. Hopefully by then Hinna would be done and then they could find Orchid.

She was ready to go home. She was almost back at the register but then I pointed her in the direction of an interesting paper weight. It was a spinning wheel.

Despite herself, she gave the wheel a whirl. It was the only thing missing in the tower she had created for herself. Safia watched the wheel spin round and round. Safia didn't know how long she had been staring at it but when she looked up Hinna was standing behind her.

"There you are," she said. "I'm ready to call it a day. What is that that you're staring at?"

Hinna's cheeks were red and her hair a little mussed as if she had just finished a vigorous walk.

Safia recalled how tired Hinna's eyes looked. How she looked at the little spinning wheel like she recognized it. Safia expected her to say, "Oh, I have one just like it," but instead her tone became irritable and indulgent at the same time.

"You've always loved these little knick knacks… it's nice," she said and then almost as an afterthought, "let me buy it for you."

Safia was about to correct her. It wasn't she who liked these trinkets. People were always confusing them, but something stopped her from pointing this out.

Safia couldn't recall what happened next or how she ended up at home. The last thing that her mind gravitated to was the moment she placed the spinning wheel on her nightstand that evening. She gave it a whirl and watched it spin in that mechanical, methodical manner that simple machines have for foraging onward. It made her think that the universe was one simple machine and the rest of us spokes and cogs, even those of us who are asleep are ornaments carved into its body. It provided some comfort.

But the machine never did stop. It kept spinning and spinning, set in its course. Safia kept this to herself, afraid that perhaps the wheel had in fact stopped and it was only her mind that kept spinning.

Safia chose not to tell him this, afraid that she would look even crazier than she already was. The spinning wheel was still on her night stand; still spinning. Instead she said, "I've been trying to sleep since I got home that evening."

"I think you'll be able to sleep very soon," he said.

"Are you sure?"

"I'm sure, because even though the last couple days have been painful, you've made progress. You've remembered. Even if you didn't want to, your mind has found a way to remember."

"I've remembered…" she said sounding skeptical.

"Safia, pull out your calendar, look closely at today's date...now circle 11 p.m."

Safia did as she was told. As she circled 11 p.m. in her day planner, a brick in the tower nudged free and Safia was able to feel as if she had made some progress.

At 11 p.m. lying in her bed, staring at the ceiling, Safia fell into a deep impenetrable sleep.

CHAPTER NINE

Alan Memorial Hospital

It was a day when all was quiet, like the days of months that passed before the sleeping girl came into their lives — devoid of any mystery or enchantment. Older patients had become better or not become better and left the ward. New patients now occupied the existing rooms, each bringing with them new challenges. The ward had become full...crowded in fact as extra beds had been put in to accommodate the influx of new patients. Perhaps, that's why she hadn't noticed him.

He blended into this place so well. Sarah had become too busy to raise an eyebrow, so she scarcely had time to pause for a break in between rolling to one task and the next. What's more, new gossip had filled the hospital corridors...co-workers getting engaged, having babies or returning from exotic holidays and pictures, pictures and pictures galore, smart phones being passed around...babel and tweets and general ruckus.

The presence of the sleeping girl seemed to have lost its allure, except for him. For everyone else, the novelty of the beautiful patient wore off and she became like any other patient. Sarah wondered if she had imagined all of it. If it was like some kind of mass hysteria that the whole department had got caught up in and now the storm had passed.

She peered inside the sleeping girl's room. It was lonely and deserted, but very ordinary. Flowers that had lost their freshness still lingered in a vase, an out of date calendar sat on the night stand. No one had bothered to remove it and off to the side behind one of the vases a curious little ornament Sarah hadn't seen before. It was a little golden spinning wheel that would turn as the breeze blew in from the window— round and round it would spin long after she left the room.

Aidan had never craved adventure. He'd never climbed a tower to save a beautiful princess, it was a nice thought, but being the hero was not all it's cracked up to be. What happened if you fell and broke your neck? Still, he would be willing to give it a go just to get out of this meeting. The boardroom felt strangely suffocating; strange because the windows were so large and expansive. As if being afraid of heights weren't bad enough, looking down could send a tremor through anyone's body causing them to look away, lest the ground crumble beneath their feet. Of course the windows would not open; at least not on the seventy-second floor—not that any of the people here had the integrity to jump!

The meeting hadn't been going anywhere for a long time now. Aidan had to suppress a desire to groan. A long, drawn out status meeting was not where he needed to be right now, not because they were mind numbing—which they were— and not because he was easily distracted—which he was—but because his mind was in a state of flux. Aidan had finally found a riddle he could not solve. Generally, he liked puzzles. Solving puzzles was what got him where he was today. But this was more than a puzzle or a game. Aidan did not want to say mid-life crisis but he could feel the words lurking at the back of his mind and he'd be damned if he'd let them reach the tip of his tongue. 'Mid-life' was a word that frightened him even more than 'bailout' and for that reason, he pretended to pay attention, letting the content of the meeting float through his head, as if it were a foreign language.

When they couldn't concentrate, the only respectable thing to do was to look down at their phones, and that at least gave the illusion of multitasking, but there was nothing in his in-box he hadn't already read a hundred times. He looked up at the faces of his colleagues; there were more than a couple glancing down at their phones. Jerry was looking up and then periodically writing things down in his planner. The bastard was probably actually taking notes, everyone else had unbuttoned the top two buttons on their shirts and rolled up their sleeves and despite the central air, their foreheads had begun to glisten. Aidan was willing to bet that no one had had more than four hours of sleep. It reminded Aidan of some sort of grotesque brotherhood; there was Morty, who was up to his ears in debt, Frank who liked to play the ponies, and Jay who just liked to play. No wonder they were sweating.

Then there was the straight shooter, the quiet guy in the corner, who didn't drink, didn't eat meat, held his own at work, saved his money—Aidan was willing to bet he had a small fortune tucked away in the Cayman Islands—and went to bed quietly at eleven-thirty every night, and somehow he looked worst of all. Aidan was sure that just knowing he had to depend on the likes of them was enough to make him chug Pepto-Bismol. Only Jerry still looked the way he did when he had come in this morning, a state that was inversely proportional to his personal life.

This unease, this boredom was new for Aidan. Aidan was used to moving quickly from challenge to challenge. Problems always had established parameters. For once Aidan had found a problem that he couldn't think his way out of; hell he couldn't even define the problem. All of this was making him slightly uncomfortable. Against his better judgment he had tried to describe his problem to Fish. Well, not so much his problem, but his state of agitation. If he were to actually describe his problem it would warrant the type of solution that might involve a strait jacket. As the Chinese have said, he was living in interesting times. The only person he might remotely be able to trust was Fish.

Fish was not the type of guy you would call a listener. He only had the one piece of advice that applied to everything and nothing, almost like a koan—but one that was created by a drunken, lecherous Zen Master. So why was Aidan babbling about what he had been feeling the last couple weeks…probably, because Fish was also the most non-judgmental guy he could go to. It made him a good lawyer and probably an even better friend. There was no telling how many clients had disclosed their sins to Fish feeling somehow purged. They sensed his appetites. Here was a guy that wouldn't judge...that couldn't judge a person.

He had to give Fish credit. Fish would listen without interrupting, look him in the eye and nod his head at all the appropriate times, he always seemed to know when someone was seeking absolution. The very nature of the counsel chosen indicated the advice someone wanted to hear.

What Aidan wanted was a distraction. Fish was not the type of guy who would solve the problems, but instead he helped Aidan forget them. Aidan felt self-conscious talking about this shit over the phone. He needed to look Fish in the eye, see the expression on his face, so he knew what he was saying didn't sound too crazy. That's why Aidan suggested meeting after work. Aidan had never felt nervous about talking to Fish before but here he was sitting in a plush coffee house wishing that he had something a little more stiff in his cup than this syrupy crap that passed for coffee. Apparently, it was a new flavor. The clerk had suggested it. When it was Aidan's turn to order he just stood there with a blank expression on his face, trying to remember why he was there in the first place, that was when she had suggested the drink. It tasted like something a child would like; fitting considering how young the barista looked. No doubt she thought he must be smitten with her, as she seemed to look back at his table a couple times.

Fish noticed her too, but fortunately for once kept his comments to himself.

As Aidan began to speak he realized he was actually beginning to sweat. He could feel the moisture under his armpits and his throat felt dry. He had meant to sound matter-of-fact, nonchalant, as if this was no more than a minor inconvenience. Instead, he came off like someone who was seriously disturbed. Aidan waited for Fish to say something to diffuse the situation. He could always count on Fish for some really 'creative' solutions and Aidan couldn't wait to see what he had in store. Perhaps, he would just laugh it off, suggest something to break the tension...parachuting, bungee jumping, a Turkish bath.

Fish gave him a very contemplative "Hmmm..." while pondering it all over.

"Maybe you're over thinking this," he said.

"What do you mean?"

"I mean, you said you feel disconnected from reality; you're having restless dreams, and you feel like you're going through a midlife crisis. Well, I've been reading Jack's book and all this sounds like a crisis of the spirit, like there's a conflict between your internal and your external self."

"Dude, are you screwing with me? Say that again with a straight face."

"What Jack is suggesting is a valid philosophical point of view."

"I'm still waiting for the gotcha..."

Instead, Fish gave him the undertaker look, the one that's reserved for clients when he has to tell them they're broke; there's no more money in the trust, the estate is up to its eyeballs in debt, and they can't pay their personal chef...secretary...masseuse.

"Seriously, you're not suggesting I listen to Jack Westland. If I listened to Jack Westland he would say something insane like...stop thinking."

"That's it, stop thinking then," he said euphorically. "Well, I'm glad we cleared that up, now we can go to this little place I've been meaning to tell you about where..."

Telling Aidan to stop thinking was like telling Aidan to stop breathing. It wasn't in his blood. He would sooner succumb to Chinese water torture or walking on coals. He wondered if that was in Jack Westland's book. "Now you're not being fair," he could hear Fish say. Still, sitting in a Wall Street boardroom trying to meditate was not how he envisioned solving his problems. Sitting in a bar wouldn't solve them either but at least you were dealing with it like a man.

Aidan took a quick look around. Jerry was still talking only now he had a PowerPoint presentation up. It was riveting material for someone like Aidan—but Aidan had always been an anomaly. At one time he would have been glued to the figures, but today he felt zombies looked more alive than this lot. He was betting that more than three-quarters of these guys were already zoned out. As long as he didn't close his eyes he would be okay. He decided to give it a try; at this point shutting down seemed like a blessing. He decided to stare at the presentation and let his mind go blank, kinda like he did when he was at the theatre or at a poetry reading or the ballet or any of the various engagements he had been dragged to in his former life.

Of course no sooner did he push one thought out of his brain than others started creeping in. Aidan tried his best to keep these thoughts PG, until he realized that if he didn't get his mind out of the gutter he was going to end up with the type of attention that he did not need. The last thing that Fish had told him to do was to concentrate on his breathing. It took another deep breath to push out the porn, one more to blow away his portfolio, his golf score, grocery list, and his dry cleaning until there were no more spiders creeping into his brain…until there was nothing left but an empty room.

It felt like Chinese water torture. It felt like he was holding his breath but then Aidan began to see something.

There is no light. Only a black tunnel and only the vaguest notion of moving, of traveling, and then the tunnel gives way to a road. The road cuts through a wooded area, foliage all around. You can hear the rustling of leaves in the wind, the chirping of crickets in the grass, and perhaps even the howling of wolves—if you really listen closely. It seems to be the type of night that warrants moonlight—if it were not for the street lamps that eclipse the bed of stars. As if tuning into the right frequency, the sound of voices becomes clearer. At first it is just a murmur; discourse perhaps from a radio in the background and then the volume increases steadily. It is not the radio but a conversation. The tone is soft at first and then begins increasing in pitch.

Everything becomes faster and as the velocity of the vehicle propels forward, the trees and the road and the woods become a blur, all the while the voices became louder and more belligerent. Speaking has turned into yelling. The road has become bumpy and jarring, a roller coaster albeit one that has gone out of control. It is unclear whether the intensity of the voices is the result of a disagreement now or fright from the terrifying journey. Yet there is no hint of slowing down...they will crash to their deaths. It is an unsettling thought but one that hangs to the recesses of the mind. The last sound, the very last sound is a blood curdling screech.

CHAPTER TEN

I am a fly on the wall.

A tiny insignificant speck of dust. It's how I like it. What better place to wait for her? A place that has long forgotten what it's like to be awake, long forgotten that it is dreaming. Yet, here I am watching…waiting. I can wait for hours…days. I've become good at it.

What a place this is. I can taste the anxiety in the air. I can smell it in their breaths; a sour smell like rotting milk. It makes me smile, all these little people waiting for me to maneuver their little lives. I raise my fingers to my lips and I blow them a deep kiss. I can see my breath shimmer through the room sparkling like glitter. It falls softly on all the inhabitants, a little shiver down their spines, a little prick in their ear and even though I cast my net wide there is only one that I hope to lure in. But will she hear my whispers?

She will be coming here soon unaware that she is the instrument of my destiny. Her eyes will need to be my eyes, her voice my voice and her limbs will walk the path I am unable to take until that moment that I receive that warm, gentle, and perfectly delicious kiss and we can both wake up.

There she is walking down a long hallway opening a forgotten door, a little hesitantly—I know the feeling. The door creaks open. The room has not been used in many years.

It's been waiting for her.

There were no more rows of cubicles, no more neighbors on the right, left and across from her. No more chatter, no more whispers of gossip in the hallway. No more smell of food, greasy lunches and mid-afternoon popcorn snacks. No more people dropping by, asking what she was working on and if she wanted to grab a coffee. No more shooting hoops through the toy basketball net at the back of the studio. No more looking over the rows of empty cubicles and seeing a familiar face when she was working late at night. The plaque outside her door now said "Art Director."

The promotion was brisk and efficient coming right after her annual review. The party was cordial and pleasant, held in a boardroom during the mid-afternoon, snacks of chips, dip, and cake. It felt like someone else's cake, like someone else's party. The congratulatory remarks did nothing to console her. Safia had a queasy feeling in her stomach, as if she was being banished, shunned from the group. Life could be lonely outside the pack and Safia could never quite picture herself a suit.

It was some consolation that it was not a brand new office. The previous tenant had left his mark, an assortment of thumbtacks on the bulletin board, the outline of where a poster once hung, chips and scratches on the wall—in truth the room could have used a coat of paint—and a bobble head doll that never made it into the final packing. Safia wondered who would leave such a bobblehead doll...the goofy grin, the giant head rolling up and down as if someone had just said something hilarious. It reminded her of looking in a Funhouse mirror, different parts of the body distorted and reflected back—giant heads, condensed torso, elongated neck. Life could never be taken too seriously with such a doll in the office. Safia stared at the bobble head doll unaware that a stranger that had just walked into her office.

"Perhaps, you should furnish these walls with samples of your work...a showcase."

Her voice was deep and rich and carried traces of the West Indies. She stood in the doorway wearing a dress made out of gray wool and a biker jacket, her thick, dark hair pulled up into a bun, her rimless glasses doing nothing to conceal the thickness of her lashes or the exquisiteness of her eyes. Safia thought she sounded almost musical. Without any introduction Safia knew who she was, had seen her walking briskly down the hallways always surrounded by people at office parties and industry events. Maya Lacasse needed no introduction.

"You're not the first creative here to feel like a fish out of water," and then seeing Safia's surprise added, "I'm sorry to sneak up on you. You just look so lost in an empty room...intimidating isn't it? You may not know this, but I started out in the Dream House."

Safia hadn't expected to meet Maya so soon. Although not the Creative Director, she was integral to the firm. Maya had gone through the ranks as a creative and been with the firm for a good ten years. She was familiar with all the firm's creative output and made recommendations on which creative to pair with each campaign. She was responsible for Safia getting promoted from Graphic Designer to Art Director. In some ways, Safia was more nervous about meeting her than the Creative Director, Blair Van Gilder.

Blair had welcomed her to the department, introduced her to all the other creatives on the floor and showed her to her office. He was not young, with snow white hair flopping casually around his face and sea blue eyes. In his exuberance, he resembled an overgrown child. He was rather fanciful, not the type of person to delve into the practicalities of running a business. No, it was Maya who was the brains behind the department and handled the business strategy. Blair's genius though was uncontested. Together they made a formidable team.

"That's actually a great idea. Who says advertising isn't art? Hopefully, it will motivate me every time I'm working on a new campaign. I can look up at my walls and remember the blood, sweat and tears that went into creating each ad."

"That's a great way to look at it. The things we create really are our babies. Well, I just dropped by to welcome you to the department. I think it's going to be a wonderful fit. You really are a gifted artist and we have some exciting new accounts where your voice and your talent are going to shine."

"Thanks," Safia said. Suddenly the knots in her stomach did not feel as tight anymore.

Safia spent the rest of the afternoon unpacking. Her first creative brief would be tomorrow morning at 10 a.m. with the suit that was handling the account and Safia wanted to be ready. She was deciding which of her ads she would hang on the wall, intuitively she thought some of her more recent pieces would be best, but there were some notable ads that she had worked on earlier in her career as well, then she heard a tap at the door. At first she thought Maya or Blaine had come back but when she turned around it was Orchid standing shyly at the entrance.

"Are we Gremlins allowed up here, or is it just suits?"

"O-M-G, do you even need to ask?" The relief that Safia felt upon seeing a familiar face was palpable.

Orchid looked around, "Nice digs, you even have a window."

If you could call it a window, thought Safia looking out into a wall of concrete. Safia could have lamented the seventy-foot building outside her window but she knew that the only thing it was blocking was a parking lot.

"Thanks, I was thinking it would make a nice frame for one of my pieces. Maybe something that provides a better view than steel and stone. "

"So, I hear you've met the Dark Queen and her Poodle," said Orchid.

"You just missed her as a matter of fact. Pray, tell me the meaning behind the name. Dark Queen seems a little cruel of a classification."

"Only, if you'll quit the medieval slang. You're getting your centuries all confused. You sound like you've been to too many Medieval Times shows."

"You mean the ones with the horses and the jousting."

"Yeah, now stop it. You're bringing back too many painful memories."

"Oh yeah, I forgot about your stint in acting...children's theater was it? I would never have pegged you for a Maid Marion. Did you..."

"Do you want to hear the rest of this, or do you want me to exit stage right now?"

"No, no. Give me the low down on the Dark Queen. I'm always up for a little intel."

Orchid rolled her eyes and groaned as if to say "enough of the weird lingo" but Safia couldn't help it. She wasn't feeling like herself today, whatever herself was supposed to feel like.

"For one," Orchid continued. "She seems to have a magic wand...and second anyone that looks up into those big brown eyes becomes putty in her hands...and third, you can't pass gas around here without her knowing about it."

"All knowing, all seeing, she must have a magic mirror."

"Mirror, mirror on the wall who's the freakiest—creative, that is—of them all?" said Neal, as he walked in and gave Safia a devilish grin.

"I think we all know who that is," said Safia

"True, I can get pretty freaky," said Neal.

"So, what do you know about the Maya...and her magic wand?"

"I know I have a wand that can perform magic in the dark…especially for a Queen."

"Ooooh," groaned Orchid.

"That's below the belt," said Safia chuckling and then coming out into full-fledged hysterics.

"Hey, it's not that funny," said Neal.

"Well, if you want to regain my respect, tell me what you've heard."

"Well, I do have my ear to the ground."

"It's not where you put your ear that we worry about," said Orchid

"What have I heard? Nothing, that's just it, no one's heard much about her. Wish I could say she was a mistress of the sweet poison, custodian of the golden handcuffs. "

"That's not quite what they mean by golden handcuffs," said Safia.

"What he means is that she's good at keeping people she likes. There are rumors of high profile creatives losing lucrative offers. Basically, she keeps you until she's done with you," said Orchid giving the bobble head doll a tap.

"What happens when she's done with you?"

"You disappear into oblivion. Every high profile creative that left Corbette never did anything notable afterwards."

A quiver went down Safia's spine. Looks like I've been had, she thought. The bobble head doll seemed to nod in agreement.

Safia sat in her new office in front of her new Mac trying not to let Orchid's words creep her out. It was different

above ground. Down in the studio—The Dream House—she had been protected by the inner workings of the firm. The designers were like little elves that worked at night, putting together dreams, hidden where no one else could see them, safe in their own world. Here, Safia was not protected by the confines of the studio. Here it was business as usual: execs interacting with each other, execs interacting with creatives, and Maya interacting with everyone. It was a strange thing to think but whenever Maya smiled it sent a shiver down her spine, as if Maya was hiding some very sharp teeth.

There was a sharp tap on the door and for a second Safia wondered if the Ice Queen hadn't been able to read her thoughts.

"Come in," called Safia a little reluctantly.

Hinna popped her head inside the door. "Am I interrupting? Boy you look a little spooked."

"Come on in," said Safia. "I was just thinking about my new boss."

If anything could add a little sweetness to Safia's mood it was Hinna. Hinna strolled in, her glossy hair hanging down her back, wide eyed and rosy cheeked and dressed in pastels…a modern day sugar plum fairy. When Hinna smiled it made Safia feel like she had just eaten chocolate.

Hinna took a seat on the couch.

"What's going on?" asked Safia

"We've decided to set a date for the engagement party. It's going to be three weeks from Saturday and I need your help, otherwise mama is going to drive me crazy."

"Maybe, I like it when she drives you crazy."

"Don't make fun and anyway you know how we fight. She won't listen to a thing I say unless you're there."

"Hinna, I just started a new job with a boss that's more than a little scary. I'm going to have my hands full."

"Please...it won't take up too much time and you may appreciate a little distraction."

"Okay...what do we need to do from now until the engagement party?"

"Let's see. I'll need your help figuring out decorations, food and of course my outfit...and your outfit. Don't worry about the guest list. We've got that covered...and there will be plenty of single guys."

"Should we start with your outfit?"

"I knew we were on the same page," said Hinna pulling out a stack of magazines both mainstream and South Asian.

"I think I want something that's a fusion of both cultures."

Two hours later they had gone through fifty magazines pulled out pages and marked them up with notes. They had also gone through half a dozen websites. Exhausted, they sat back and examined their work.

"This was a great start," said Hinna. "Now we need to book a date and check out the boutiques."

Safia tried not to grimace; this was going to be a full day event. Fortunately, Hinna was booked next weekend. If according to her the engagement plans were just getting started, she wondered how much work the wedding was going to be.

"Do you want to go get some dinner?" Hinna asked. "I feel bad for taking up so much of you're your time. Let me at least feed you," said Hinna giving Safia a warm molasses smile.

Safia was about the reply that she was exhausted when there was a knock at the door.

"Come in," she said a little wearily. It was Neal and Orchid.

"Hey, what's going on guys?" asked Orchid.

"We're just thinking about going out for dinner," said Hinna

"Then we came just in time. We know a great new place that opened up couple blocks from here called Asmara."

"Ooh," said Hinna her eyes lighting up. "I think I've heard of that place. Doesn't it have Middle Eastern inspired tapas?"

"That's the one."

"I have been dying to try that out."

"I was really thinking of making this an early night," Safia started to say knowing that with Neal around, this evening was not going to end after dinner.

"Don't be a stick in the mud," Said Orchid. "Grab your purse."

The walls were decorated with Middle Eastern tapestries, landscape paintings hung on the walls and ornate hookahs (tobacco pipes) were fitted in various corners. A lilt of incense infused the air and boots were lined in rich red velvet. When Aidan arrived she was already waiting for him. Her hair had been let down and it just grazed her shoulders. She always wore light make-up but today she had added a rich copper lipstick she always wears on her "nights out." Today she was wearing a long burgundy kurta (tunic) and skinny jeans. In her simplicity she looked extremely exotic and years younger than her actual age. She caught his eye as he stood adjusting to the light in the doorway and waved him over. It never ceased to amaze him how different his mother seemed when she was not standing next to his father.

Aidan made his way over to the booth and kissed her on her cheek and she smiled giving him a menu. "I hope you brought your appetite," she said, "because there are so many things I want to try."

It had been a long time since Aidan had had dinner with his mother like this. Amina had always been his father's favorite and he had always had better rapport with his mother. Aidan looked at the menu; it was really Middle Eastern fusion. They started with some spicy dates—with goat cheese, pistachio, cranberry-harissa—and quickly ordered more tapas. His mother had obviously been studying the menu for awhile and he let her take the lead.

Eating always made him feel more relaxed and he saw it had a similar effect on his mother. They were alike in many ways. Neither of them were delicate eaters. They both chomped on their food, and with a mouth full of spinach falafel, she proceeded to tell him about her shopping expedition in the city—that's when he noticed the colorful bags she was hoarding under the booth—and the latest gossip about her friends and her friend's children. She paused taking a sip from her drink to ask, "I'm not chewing your ear off, am I?"

The older Aidan got the more he enjoyed those rare occasions when he got to hang out with his mother. The more he could glimpse what she had been like before she married his father. Without his father they were more like friends...equals. "Not at all," he said in between bites of Tamarind beef—with smoky eggplant puree and pine nuts. "I am fascinated by Pinky auntie's lack of skill at coordinating her accessories with her outfits after spending all this time in the latest boutiques."

"You're making fun of me," she said grinning and reaching for some lamb ribs.

"I'm serious. No one ever talks about this at work. My female friends are mostly all married and Amina...well Amina may as well be a guy."

"That's a horrible thing to say about your sister," she said laughing out loud.

"I won't tell her if you don't. Besides whom else do you have for girl talk?"

It was true. Amina—like his father—would rather be talking batting averages and touchdowns.

"You're a good son, but there's something else I wanted to talk to you about."

"Mom," he began to groan.

"Humor me. I'm your mother and I worry about you. There are quite a few parties coming up this season that our family is invited to. I want you to promise me that you will make an appearance."

"I'll try," he said pulling out the dessert menu. The restaurant had gotten significantly busier than when he had walked in. A large group had just come through the door and the waiter was putting together tables. Aidan didn't mind admitting it but the best date he had had in a long time had been with his mother.

"Now, how about a baked Alaska for dessert?" asked his mother.

CHAPTER ELEVEN

I enter like a gust of wind.

Like the wind, I am everywhere and nowhere. I watch from the corners. It is like standing over a dollhouse, only I am so close I can smell yesterday's breakfast. I can smell more than that, I can smell the food...the drink, and the smoke, the flavored tobacco, the reefer and the other intoxicants from days and weeks ago that have seeped in and clung to their blood.

I love parties and I will be with them tonight listening to their conversations and maneuvering their words. I like these settings best when masks fall to the floor and then I need only whisper in their ears. I will blow someone a kiss, it will tickle his neck and he will look at the person beside him. They will think it is the drink, but it's really me.

Still, she will know better. She knows better than they do. She will feel me. She will know that I am here. She will look over her shoulder as her eyes dart from person to person. She doesn't know who she is looking for but soon she will find him.

She doesn't know it yet, but she is waiting for someone. She thinks she's here with her friends. She thinks she is here for a gathering but it is really me who has sent for her. He will be there soon.

She will need to pay attention…for the both of us.

On Safia's way out of the office a couple more people latched onto their group with Neal and Orchid at the front and Hinna hanging back, flirting animatedly with a cute designer. Soon they had quite a big dinner party. When they reached the restaurant it was full, still the waiters were willing to pull together a few more tables for them. Six people squeezed in next to each other.

"Well, this is cozy," said Hinna with a giggle. Of course Hinna was sitting beside a guy that could have been a model for a rugged Ken doll. Safia had one of the designers from the studio on one side of her and Neal on the other with Orchid sitting directly across from them.

Sitting this close to Neal made Safia's hair stand on end, but at least he wasn't directly in front of her. She wouldn't know where to look. As it was, she could feel his arm graze her whenever each of them shifted a little. She could smell his cologne, which was musky and a little too strong. There was no denying, she was sitting next to the big bad wolf. Just to have something to concentrate on Safia picked up the menu. As everyone settled in the waitress came up to them and a round of drinks were ordered—it would only be the beginning.

Safia closes her eyes for a second and feels something against her cheek, a tickle...an invisible kiss, someone watching her. It occurs to Safia that she has been watched carefully for several years, her parents, her shrink...sometimes even her. A wave of calm goes through her as she thinks of her sister. It's a breakthrough surely to feel calm and not guilt. When she opens her eyes the waitress is taking their dinner order and everyone is blurting out tapas that they want to try.

Just the mention of food makes her stomach growl. Soon their table is lined with exotic dishes: fried cauliflower, lamb tagine, fried mussels, fava bean pate, and seven-layer hummus.

Safia wants to dig-in to her heart's content but something bothered her. Call it intuition...call it an itch that couldn't be scratched.

Safia looked around the room but couldn't identify anything out of place. The restaurant was full of small quiet parties. She sees a man and a woman seated toward the back of the restaurant start to make their way out. The man is tall wearing a camel colored coat and his hair is thick and dark. She isn't able to see his face. The woman is petite, but elegant. Her eyes stay on them until they leave. Long after they are gone, Safia keeps staring at the door where they last stood as if they are still there, as if they have left an imprint...like ghosts. It is Orchid's voice that punctures her thoughts.

"Safia, you barely have anything on your plate," said Orchid.

Safia began filling her plate with hummus and fried cauliflower.

"Let me help you there," said Neal passing over some lamb and asking the waitress to refill her drink.

Several courses appeared and disappeared. They finished dinner with coffee and a hookah with raspberry flavored tobacco. One whiff of hookah is like inhaling ten cigarettes at the same time…instant buzz. The hookah started getting passed around and everyone took long drags, and finally it was Safia's turn. She looked at the ornate gold pipe. It reminded her of Aladdin's lamp and she wondered if there was a genie in there waiting for them to smoke him out.

Safia closes her eyes and takes a deep drag. She can feel the smoke, as if it is alive with intent, go into her mouth, down her throat, and into her lungs. It was not content to stay there so it rises up and stings her eyes. She can't breathe and she can't see anything and she is taken back to a place she doesn't want to go. It finally exits her and Safia has come up for air, and she is left in a coughing fit. Neal is patting her on the back. The hookah has been passed on to someone else but Safia can still see that invisible smoke rising into the air and vanishing out the window.

Alan Memorial Hospital

Someone has left a little music on and the soft, classical melody infiltrates the girl's room. Her expression seems calm, content but then it always looks like that. Quietly, Sarah combs her hair and wipes her down with a damp cloth subtly changing her position so that she doesn't get bedsores. She never gets bedsores. Her skin always looks smooth, never sweaty, and never dirty. There is a soft fragrance that Sarah has begun to notice, a dewy morning smell...like spring. It sounds crazy even to her and she wonders if she's been imagining it, but then she has only to remind herself of how everyone has secretly adopted the girl to know she's not imagining it.

She has more fresh flowers than any other patient. Staff secretly visit her and murmur words of encouragement. No one can pass by this room without the urge to look inside. She has truly become their princess...and the music. The soft melody has begun to crescendo.

Is she listening to the music? Sarah wonders. The symphony with its soft droplets of notes, like rain water, seems to be speaking to her. Sarah imagines that she wants to answer back. She imagines that her lips long to form words that are as melodious as the notes themselves. Inadvertently Sarah begins to hum along with the music. She rarely does this anymore. She can't remember why. Just being with the girl has brought within her a sense of calm. The expression on the girl's face looks far away as if she is somewhere else, as if she is dreaming. The music seems to be calling her back, hanging on to her like a desperate hand, not willing to let her go.

In a few minutes Sarah will be done and she'll move on to the next task. She looks at the girl; it almost feels as if they have been conversing...a silent conversation where each person's loneliness speaks and responds to the other.

It is midnight Aidan is in his apartment. He looks at his hand; a slight tremor. There is a part of him that is still shaking. He is beyond wound up and he picks up his phone. There are a couple texts from Fish and a hundred emails from work. Aidan is surprised he hasn't had to go back to the office. Aidan gives Fish a call. He sounds drunk and in the middle of something. He is sober enough to let him know that Jack is leading a meditation session at a yoga studio next week and tickets are selling like hotcakes. Five winners will also get a free copy of his book and one lucky winner will get a life coaching session with Jack. That sounds rich, thinks Aidan.

Aidan starts taking deep breaths and wondering if he needs valium or something. That's probably what a shrink would tell him. The funny thing is that he is surprisingly calm. He was feeling almost normal, almost should he dare say, happy and having a nice dinner with his mother. He replays the events after they left the restaurant.

He was driving his mother home, a path he knew by rote. The roads were smooth; the traffic was all clear until it wasn't. One minute he was chatting with his mother about why it's so hard to meet the right person in this day and age and the next minute the crisp highway had disappeared.

They were barreling down a dirt road, branches hitting his windshield. He is driving a runaway car that is barreling out of control. Smoke fills his lungs and stings his eyes. He wants to brake but nothing happens. He wants to look over to his mother, but he is paralyzed and then he sees her shimmering in the darkness like a ghost. The girl he knows so well. He wants to smile. She is the compass that he has to focus on. After what seems like an eternity he's back on the sleek freeway that he knows so well. Once again she has evaporated into thin air.

His mother's a little irritated with him. "Are you paying attention?" she asks.

She thinks he's zoned out. Aidan thinks he's going to have a heart attack.

"Yeah Mom, I'm with you. I do think Pinky and her husband are a perfect match, but I gotta say looks can be deceiving. Look at you and Dad."

Now he realizes that he's gone too far.

"Dad and I don't count. Our marriage was practically arranged."

Finally, they reach his parent's quaint little suburb. He pulls into the driveway feeling like he just got off the highway to hell. He's taking deep breaths. His mother notices this and invites him to crash in his old room. As tempting as it sounds there is no way he wants to face his family at the breakfast table, in case the drive home comes up. Fortunately, his return to the city is smooth sailing, he owns the road but he still can't stop shaking.

At least now there is no pretense of being scared shitless. He doesn't stop shaking until he pops a couple sleeping pills and gets into his bed. As he drifts off to sleep he can smell a faint perfume and he knows she will be waiting for him.

Is this a dream? he wonders.

CHAPTER TWELVE

I wish that I could smile.

How pretty my angelic face would look with just a hint of a smile, delicate lips the color of a rich wine and perhaps some pink in my cheek—and yet how deceiving. It is not for lack of trying. A smile is what I desire and yet no matter how I try and cannot contort my cold lips in the slightest. I shall remain serene on the outside. I am giddy on the inside.

I have done it. I have found my knight in shining armor. I have found my Prince. I have taken a still warm dream and sent it into the waking world inch by inch...breath by breath, but not without its purpose. I have sent it with a mission, I have watched it take hold, I have watched it beckon, and now all I need is a kiss.

Just one sweet, luscious kiss would redeem me. It is enough to make me to laugh. I would like to laugh until I cry because if this is my only hope than I am doomed. I may as well resign myself to an eternity of living inside a dream and become forever a sleeping doll, but I see the old woman again...I hear her whispers in my ear. In fact, I cannot make them stop and quietly I am consoled.

I can smell him, all of him the way his aftershave intermingles with his cologne, the way the perspiration on his skin clings to the fabric of his suite. He will serve my purpose very well indeed. Look at those sad, puppy dog eyes. I want to reach out and smooth his hair, touch his cheek...stroke his hair, but this is the easy part. I lick my lips in preparation for the nibble I'd like to take. I feel something buzzing in my ears. It is my own laughter ringing hysterically inside my head.

Safia is standing outside the auditorium, ticket in hand and Hinna is nowhere to be seen. Leave it to Hinna to be late when she's already freaking out. People are going in and finding their seats. Everyone is excited, except Safia. Safia is trying not to think about work.

Since becoming Art Director Safia decided to forgo her hippy wardrobe. She left to meet Hinna and caught a reflection of herself. She wore a camel colored vest on top of a short sleeved dress shirt. At least now when she was one-on-one with Maya she would look like a professional. Safia stood nervously outside the auditorium. When Hinna tapped her on the shoulder, Safia nearly jumped.

"Sorry, I'm late. Didn't you get my text? Gosh, aren't you jumpy."

"Don't know why but I think my Creative Director has it in for me. Anyways let's take our seats."

They walked into the crowded auditorium. Hinna had brought her copy of Jack Westland's book, "The Secret to the

Universe; The Secret to You," hoping to get it signed. "This is the type of stuff that can transform your life," she said.

There was an expectant energy in the air as if everyone was waiting to be let in on a huge secret. Hinna felt antsy and they hustled to the front to get good seats.

Safia tried to control her nerves. She doesn't know why she's feeling so jittery. Yes, she does. It's because she can feel something looking over her shoulder and it makes her want to barricade herself in her apartment. She really hopes that this is the last favor she is going to have to do for Hinna, but we both know that's not true. She is not good with strangers and she hates crowds. Hinna knows this but it doesn't stop her from dragging Safia to the most uncomfortable event possible. What's the point in having a fiancé if you're always hanging out with me? Safia wants to ask, but we both know she won't. She can just imagine the hurt look on Hinna's face, the way her lower lip would slightly tremble.

Instead she says, "I don't know if this is such a good idea."

"It's just that I think this would be good for us."

"Us?"

"I mean me. It will help me keep my identity while being a couple and you have a lot to gain from this seminar as well. It might help you change your life; besides this guy is huge. This session was sold out in an hour!"

"I doubt it," mumbles Safia, "Besides my life is fine. I don't need to change my life," but it sounds weak and desperate even to her.

"Safia you live like a hermit. When are you going to come out of this dream world," says Hinna and then a little more softly, "just give this guy a chance."

It is almost controlled chaos. The auditorium is full. They've only been marketing Jack Westland a couple of months, but the turnout is huge. Hundreds of people signed up for an inspirational talk and meditation session with Jack Westland. The venue could only accommodate fifty people at a time so they've extended the dates. Fish is so excited dollar signs could be seen in his eyes and Aidan thinks there might even be a shot that he could recover some of what he lost in the economic meltdown.

Aidan is here early casing the place. He can almost feel the electricity in the air as if a rock star is about to take the stage. Self-help is the new religion for the modern yuppie world. Aidan sees Jack walk into the auditorium. He gives Aidan a tentative smile. Aidan's nerves are all jumbled, he's almost afraid that he's going to have an out of body experience in a minute or two, but Jack looks serene. Aidan walks over to Jack. Until now, he's always avoided speaking directly to him, letting Fish be the middleman.

"How are you doing? Ready for the big session?" Asked Aidan.

"I can't lie. I feel like I'm riding a wave," says Jack. Aidan suppresses the urge to grown.

"It feels good though. It feels like we're tapping into the universe. I think we're going to help a lot of people today.

Help some people find peace," says Jack looking Aidan in the eye.

Aidan wants to tell him to stuff it, but instead says,

"Dude, I have peace coming out of my ears," which sounds dumb even to him.

"We both know that, that's not true. You seem restless, even haunted. Fish may not notice but I can tell that something's been eating you, but we're going to work through this brother. Hopefully, starting today," he says putting a hand on Aidan's shoulder.

Aidan doesn't know what to say, maybe to be relieved that someone like Jack Westland has figured out what a freak he is. Fortunately for Aidan, he does not need to say anything. Jack is off preparing notes, shaking hands, and getting ready for the talk. Aidan takes a seat and watches people coming in when he spots a familiar face. He almost misses it but there it is peering through the crowd. Their eyes meet and now Aidan knows for sure that he's been spotted as well.

This is awkward. Aidan is not sure what he's going to say. They don't even know each other that well but before Aidan has time to think he is standing face to face with Jerry Eackland, the VP at his firm.

"Hey, wow. I never expected to see you here," says Aidan

"I gotta tell you…I never expected to be here myself but then something woke up in me and I realized that it was time."

"Time?"

"Yeah, time to move on; time to get my life back in order. I haven't told anyone yet but I'm also going to be resigning from the firm. It's just not me anymore. I'm going to do something totally different, not sure what yet but I know it's going to be great?

"Wow, man that's fantastic," said Aidan. "Let me know where you end up. Just drop me a line from wherever you are."

"I will," holding out his hand so they can shake.

After Jerry makes his way to his seat Aidan is floored and the show hasn't even started yet. This time when Jack takes the stage Aidan finds that he is actually listening. It doesn't mean that he actually believes anything that Jack is saying but it's been twenty minutes and Aidan has not tuned him out, and that's got to mean something.

Aidan looks around; people are following Jack's recommendations. They are taking deep breaths. Aidan does the same. He finds his mind is very still, so still that he can almost see her. It is like trying to see someone in the dark and concentrating on the haze causes them to become clearer and clearer. He knows that she is waiting for him but just as he is about to reach out to her, he is brought back to the present by a crowd of people quickly moving past him.

When he looks up, Jack is bombarded by people who want autographs; that is why he notices her. She is the only one in a row of empty seats. Her eyes are closed, her hair is loose and she is wearing a beige sweater that compliments her coloring. She appears to be in deep thought, concentrating on something the rest of them can't hear. She doesn't feel like a stranger and Aidan has the inexplicable urge to go up to her.

As he comes closer he sees that her features are delicate, her eyes deep set and her lips...perfectly kissable. She has been waiting for him oblivious to the commotion around her. He tries get to her as quickly as possible but there are too many people in his way, too many people rushing past him to try and get to Jack.

He is now pushing past the crowd; it is like going the wrong way on and escalator. A big man nearly knocks him over and he thinks he is going to fall but he feels someone grasp his shoulder and steady him. When Aidan looks up again she is gone. Standing above him is Fish with a big grin on his face, "Did I tell you this guy was great or what?"

Alan Memorial Hospital

It was a full moon this evening. The fullest, brightest moon hanging in the sky. It gave Sarah a strange feeling of displacement just looking at it. Under the moonlight, the sleeping girl looked almost ghostly, her skin reflecting a strange luminescent sheen.

When Sarah touched her hand it felt frightfully cold. It made a shiver go down her spine and for a frightful moment Sarah was scared that the girl might not be with them in the morning. As Sarah swallowed down her fears, she became overcome with the earthy flavor of nutmeg. It is the old woman that is responsible for this.

She had come today, slightly hunched over, wearing her pale sari, her withered hands carrying two big boxes of Indian mehtai for the staff. She had smiled as she handed them to the head nurse, but it was a sad, mournful smile. When they opened the box they saw colorful cubes of sugar, butter and exotic spices that reminded Sarah of fudge—just as rich, and just as decadent. Sarah had one and then another to curb her anxiety, and each time she took a bite, she thought this must be something the sleeping girl liked to eat…why else would the old woman have brought it?

Sarah had no doubt that the box of sweets would be finished quickly; everyone was always hungry here. Whenever anyone asked who brought the box? Sarah would respond that it was the coma patient's family and then a realization would hit them that these came from the sleeping girl, as if the old woman was just the messenger. It was a crazy thought that somehow the sleeping girl had personally picked these out for them, hand picking all the different flavors.

It was only on a night like this in the eerie moonlight that Sarah could entertain a thought like this and surely, the sunrise would wash all this nonsense away.

CHAPTER THIRTEEN

I woke up today…with a jolt.

I opened my eyes and I saw his face staring back at me. I am aglow. I have looked into his eyes, felt his beating heart. I have flown with him across the night sky and buried my face in his chest. I felt his every breath as if I were breathing it myself, and the beating of his heart inside my body and the wind blowing through our hair.

There is somewhere I want to take him, somewhere where I know he will find me, but I must lead the way. He is waiting for me. I see him confused, picking at his food with his eyebrows furrowed. 'Don't look so glum,' I want to say— an opportunity has arisen, a delightful little stroke of luck.

I couldn't have planned it better myself. A path that will lead him to me, and like a good little prince he is following my trail. He is hacking away through the mad growth of vines, the enormous shrubs, the poisonous flowers, and all the foliage that encompasses me. I can hear him coming even from a place as dreary as my bed, his footsteps are music to my ears. As each branch falls, the path strengthens and becomes more resolute.

That is the one thing you cannot deny about prophecies, that no matter how long you've slept or how winding the road, they always come true.

I can see how it will end...and it will be with a kiss.

Aidan had to admire Fish's ability to talk and eat at the same time. Why let a mouthful of food get the better of a conversation? They were seated in a food court in the middle of lunch time, surrounded by people in suits partaking in mall cuisine. Fish was lapping up a dish of messy Chinese food...noodles, fried rice, and what looked to be sweet and sour chicken. Fish held the noodles in his chopsticks precariously as they engaged in conversation. Aidan didn't know how he was doing it. Surely with this much sauce one might require the use of a bib. Aidan took a bite of his own salad nicoise.

The Jack Westland campaign was going great and Fish was excited. He held his chopsticks in the air like a weapon as he spoke. They were on the verge of something big. They just needed to think bigger. They needed a professional. A professional what? Aidan wanted to ask.

"I'm glad you asked," Fish chimed in without missing a beat. Mind reading had always been Fish's best trait. "I think we need a marketing and PR firm to take us to the next level."

"The next level...?"

"Absolutely and I know the perfect shop, are you ready for it…Corbette Advertising."

"Corbette Advertising…really? That place is huge. This is going to cost us a fortune."

"Look, I know a guy, it won't be so bad. Let's just say he owes me a big favor. Now I've set up a meeting between you and a couple of execs at the agency."

"Why me?"

"A pretty boy like you will do much better with that crowd…Oh, and Jack will be there too."

Of course he will, thought Aidan.

"Do me a favor though, let me scope these people out before Jack gets there. You're the Man," said Fish.

It was like stepping into an oasis in the middle of the city. If Aidan didn't know any better, he would have thought he had stumbled into a luxury spa, what with all the marble and granite, and indoor trees. The cool blues with splashes of color seemed to say, "We're here to work hard and have fun. We don't take ourselves too seriously." Or at least that's what they want people to believe.

The large silver letters above reception that boldly stated Corbette Advertising told him he was in the right place. Aidan gave the receptionist his name. She looked like they had pulled her out of a modeling agency and of course she was probably the perkiest person he had ever met. They were expecting him and he was sent right on up to the third floor.

On the third floor he was met by the Director of Client Services, a surprisingly regular looking guy with a pleasant handshake named Gavin. He introduced Aidan first to the Creative Director, Blair Van Gilder, who with his silver hair and upper crust features looked like the type of person that could be seen wearing one of those smoking jackets that are only seen in movies and dangling an Ashton cigar from the side of his mouth. Oh yeah, one more thing, holding a brandy. Now the picture in Aidan's head was complete.

Blair vigorously shook Aidan's hand when they were introduced and he looked like he might even want to reach out and hug him. Next was his second in command Maya LaCasse who looked more like model turned socialite in her designer suit, three-inch heels, and ample curves. She had a smile that oozed sex and a handshake that was all steel. Aidan wondered who Fish's guy was. If he had to guess it would be Blair.

After introductions were made and Gavin spewed a brief speech on how happy they were that Aidan was considering their firm. Aidan started the discussion by stressing what a tight budget they were on. The look on their faces indicated that they had heard this before. Of course, he thought. Who goes into an agency and says money is no object?

As the meeting progressed he had to admit their presentation options were not as off the mark as he had expected. They would need to be reined in a little bit but many of their concepts were very workable and the subway advertising seemed really on the mark. Forty-five minutes later Jack and a couple others from the agency joined in and Jack fortunately got a watered down presentation of what Aidan had received and of course the appropriate oohing and awing over a pseudo celebrity. Jack's ego had been appropriately stroked and he was on board with the larger plan. Now what they had to do was to etch out some of the detail.

Inadvertently, Safia had started referring to the building as the stone castle. Perhaps because it looked like it came out of a fairy tale and perhaps because her sister lay sleeping there like a princess. It had been years since she had gone there to visit her sister. For now she was content to watch it from across the street knowing that her sister inhabited the seventh floor, but even as Safia would sit talking to her shrink in that same building, she could always feel her sister's presence inhabiting the floors just above her.

Today Safia was content to absorb herself in the antics of the Dream House. She had missed being here. All of the workstations were out in the open. Some of the designers had on headphones drowning out noise and plugging in some inspiration. For several minutes Safia was content to stand in the corner and watch. She noticed that her old workstation had been assigned to someone else and although its new inhabitant was not there, there were the telltale signs of it being occupied: a coffee mug, a sweater thrown over a chair, the odd post-it note on the wall. It was Tyson that noticed her first.

Tyson had her blonde hair scrunched up into a bun, which she did when she was stressed to prevent herself from clawing at it. She wore a soft, oversized sweater in heather gray above a tight fitted T-shirt and black dress pants. When she saw Safia, the first thing she did was give her a hug.

"I'm glad you've come down to visit. Are they treating you well?"

"So far they're great, but it's not like being in the Dream House."

Out of the corner of her eye she could see Neal engrossed in a conversation with another designer and it looked like Orchid had also managed to stumble into work, carrying a venti coffee and wearing shades at 9 a.m. When they saw Safia they waved her over.

"You look almost as tired as me," said Orchid.

"Hinna's wedding on top of my regular job is really wearing me out and we're still only at the engagement party stage.

"When it is it?"

"This weekend."

"OMG, I've seen your sketches. It's going to be beautiful. Take lots of pictures."

"I know, it's going to be breathtaking, and it's going to be perfect but most of all it's going to be over. I can't wait to have my life back," said Safia stifling a yawn.

"How are the suits treating you?" asked Neal.

"Good, that reminds me I'm in a meeting in five minutes. A new account, a person this time…it's supposed to be interesting. At least that's what I've been promised."

"Someone famous?" Asked Neal.

"Maybe," said Safia curious for the first time. She had never had to work on a campaign for a person before. It couldn't be worse than working on Hinna's engagement.

When she found out, her first thought was, Hinna is going to die. She would probably explode with excitement when she found out who Safia's new client was. Everybody loved this guy. Safia's head was a buzz and she wasn't even a fan but Hinna...Hinna was completely in love with Jack Westland. Not to mention if the campaign went well it would be a huge compliment to Safia's portfolio. Only a couple weeks and she was thinking like a suit already.

Of course Safia wouldn't really be dealing with Jack Westland directly. She would be working with the agency's account executive and Jack Westland's PR guy. As Safia studied the brief she began jotting down notes. She really wanted this campaign to go well. It was bad enough to screw up a product image, let alone how much worse it would be to screw up a person's image. Why was she thinking like this? Her work was always stellar. I won't shrink from a challenge, she thought.

Looking again at the brief Safia debated whether or not to use Jack Westland's picture in the campaign. She began by reviewing all the literature she had on the modern day guru and looked at testimonials from people who had read his book. Personally, Safia always liked motivational speakers and wondered what it would be like to meet him in person.

Safia looked at her calendar. She would need to get as much done as possible in the next couple of days as she was leaving early on Friday, thanks to Hinna's engagement party. As Safia's mind drifted to the preparations of Hinna's party that highlighted Safia's talents as much as any campaign, the phone began to ring. It was the tailor. Alterations to Safia's dress for the party were complete. Safia asked him to send it to Corbette.

Alan Memorial Hospital

Lately, she is almost never alone. Friends, relatives, random patients, and even staff have come to visit speaking with her for a good amount of time and coming out purged. It is happening more frequently now. Like a priestess she is hearing all of their confessions—all of their secrets.

Sarah can see it in their faces as they exit the sleeping girl's room, a sense of release from whatever has been holding them back and blocking them from moving forward. There is something about the girl's silence that invites people to speak, if only to soften the quiet. There is something in her face and in her expression that conveys patience and empathy, so that no matter how long it takes someone to tell their story she will be right there waiting...listening.

At first when speaking to her it is awkward and embarrassing as if speaking to a doll, but the more someone tells her the harder it is to stop. Sarah has seen it, people sitting and confessing for hours, wiping the perspiration from their forehead. It reminds her of an interrogation as if the girl in the bed were not so delicate, so beautiful and so obviously asleep. Sarah knows this because she has felt it too—the pull that takes hold of you.

It happens when you least expect, you could be fluffing her pillow or giving her a sponge bath or even just reading to her from a magazine when you feel it. It feels as if she has pinpointed something inside you and is now trying to coax it out. All of your walls seem to crumble until there is nothing else to do but start speaking, to start speaking about a past you no longer want to think about. That's when Sarah begins to gasp and with a deep breath runs out of the room—still not ready to divulge her secrets.

CHAPTER FOURTEEN

I am invincible.

I hold his hand tightly and pull him into my world. This is where I reign amongst dreams and nightmares. Is he afraid? I feel his blood run cold with terror while mine runs hot with desire. There is so much farther we need to go. This is only the beginning. We shall go farther than he ever imagined.

For the first time I feel the tiniest twinge of doubt, but it is a mere droplet against my skin. Still, it is there. I take another breath. I see something from the past. I see it as clearly as if it were in front of me. It makes me smile. Some might say that my smile is cold, but today my smile must be ice. It even makes me shiver.

We are getting closer. See how the wheel spins and then of course darkness, a darkness so palpable that it chokes you. I can feel it coming. I smell something too. It is a familiar scent, as familiar as the rough earth, though I will never get used to it. It is as familiar as one's hopes when they turn to ash and as familiar as one's nightmares that know exactly how to haunt you. I want to close my eyes as I feel the blackness coming, blackness so dark you fear you will never see light again—and then I hear someone scream.

It was a sharp piercing scream and like nails on a chalkboard, it punctured the silence. Aidan gasped a little as he woke up. He looked at his surroundings. His clothes were damp and wrinkled. It was past midnight. He had fallen asleep on the couch in his office. This working two jobs was really taking its toll. Fish needed to start pulling his weight a little more.

Aidan tried to remember what had woken him up. It was likely the scream of an ambulance or a police car whizzing by to the next calamity. He was working on the marketing plan for the Jack Westland project, how much was it all going to cost? And would they make enough in seminars and book sales? He had drifted off and there she was waiting patiently for him.

It was time to admit that she was real. For months now he had attributed these dreams to stress, hallucinations or even some kind of psychosis because as harrowing as this reality was, the alternative was even more unsettling, but she was real and she was trying to tell him something. It had taken a long time for him to understand this, but it wasn't until he saw the girl at the seminar, sitting quietly with her eyes closed, that he couldn't ignore that little voice at the back of his mind screaming. The resemblance was uncanny, frightening even like watching a dream leak into reality. It was a dazzling neon sign that even the darkest piece of shade, was hard to ignore.

This presented a problem and not one that Aidan was adept at solving. He went home showered, chugged some coffee, and then he closed his office door. He dialed a number. There was only one person who was able to handle how kooky he was, and not just as an adult, but for all those years as a dorky kid. She was the only one who found his weirdness endearing...thank God. He didn't know how he was going to position this but he gave it his best shot. After an awkward beginning he finally posed his question the best way he knew how.

"Have you ever had a premonition?"

"What kind of premonition?" asked his mother. "Your grandmother used to get them all the time. She could always tell when bad news was coming."

"I mean something a little more dramatic than that, maybe kind of a déjà vu. You know that you've seen it before, a person or a place."

"Are you feeling okay, Jannu?"

"I'm feeling fine Mom, but I have this nagging feeling at the back of my mind that I'm supposed to meet someone soon."

"But that's wonderful. It's what we've all been praying for."

"It's not that simple. I've got this picture in my head that I can't get rid of."

"Please tell me Jannu that you are not looking for a model, because looks aren't everything."

"Give me some credit, Mom. I'm not a shallow kid anymore this is more than that…it's, it's a premonition of sorts. I can't explain it."

"Well then listen to your voice dear and do what you need to do, and speaking of meeting people, will we be seeing you Friday?"

"I don't know. I'm working two jobs and…and…and."

"Enough with the ands, your father and I are expecting you there and we've already RSVP'd for the whole family. It's going to be a wonderful party. Now, more than ever I believe that you should come. It might be just what you need."

There was no point in arguing with his mother when she had that tone of voice. The best he could do was promise that he wouldn't come too late. Maybe he would make an appearance. Things were busy at work but calm; the markets were holding steady. Aidan logged in to check sales of Jack's book. Sales were good; they were progressively increasing.

Perhaps Fish was right, perhaps this agency would take them to a new level. Gavin, the account executive that he was working with, seemed solid. Then there was Maya Lacasse. Now there was a wild card if he ever saw one. The first time he shook hands with her he felt the hairs on his neck stand on end. It wasn't just because she was hot, he had felt that too, it was the feeling that Maya Lacasse only looked out for Maya Lacasse. He had asked Fish if he had met Maya yet.

"No but it sounds like she's right up my alley," Fish had replied.

It figured Fish wasn't happy unless he had a shark on his tale and Maya Lacasse had sharp teeth, even he knew that.

Aidan's mother looked at her phone for a few second before she put it away, a dark lock fell across her forehead. It was only when she was worried or upset that her true age could be deciphered. She had always had a fierce streak of protectiveness towards her sensitive little boy. A quality that he seemed to have diminished over the last couple years, that is until now.

Was that really her son she was talking to? He sounded so unsure of himself. So much like the little boy he used to be. It was refreshing in a way because it meant that he was looking at things differently. He was such an awkward child it had taken so long for him to come into his own, but then his career had skyrocketed. Even his father—who had always wanted Aidan to go into engineering—had to grudgingly accept his career path.

Although everyone had been thrilled when Aidan had gotten engaged, there was something about Aidan's fiancé that made her think twice. It wasn't just that her daughter, Amina, couldn't stand her. They were both fiercely competitive and used to being center-stage. It was that his former fiancé most of the time never bothered to look below the surface of anyone including Aidan. Asiya always felt that his fiancé had never broken through to the real Aidan. She had fallen for the idea, the image of Aidan and he had fallen in love with the idea of her and when that image began to crumble, so did their relationship.

Asiya looked at her watch; it was almost time for the party. She had to pick out something to wear. She eyed a cream-colored saris. Men always had it easy, she thought finally deciding on a dark-colored suit that would do nicely for her husband.

She hoped Aidan came to the party today. If Aidan did not show up today, she was sure that his father would notice. Asiya had felt the strain of their relationship for quite some time now like a taut rubber band ready to break.

Alan Memorial Hospital

There were times when Sarah couldn't distinguish between dreams and reality. When her dreams were so real, so vivid that it took several moments after she awoke to understand that what she had seen had not actually happened. This was one such dream.

It wasn't unusual for her to dream about the hospital, but it always appeared as a vague shadowy building, a fuzzy blur of sounds and images. This time it had been as real as day and lingered in her brain as crisp as any memory.

She was working the night shift and it was quiet. She was walking down the hall and she could feel someone following her. There was no noise and no footsteps and no indication from her backwards glances that there was anyone there at all, only a sense of being watched...perhaps even studied. It was only when she got back to her station and while filling out a form when she looked up. There, the sleeping girl stood before her, looking at her, mute.

She is in her white hospital gown, her hair is disheveled and her eyes and expression are blank as if she is a zombie, as if she is sleep-walking. Sarah can't tell if she comprehends what she is seeing.

"What are you doing out of bed?" Sarah can hear herself saying and then she wakes up. She wonders if she had stayed asleep longer would the girl have answered. Would Sarah have taken her by the hand and guided her back to her room? Or would the girl lunge at her, wrapping her delicate hands around Sarah's throat? Sarah doesn't know why she thinks this may be a possibility. The dream haunts her during the day like an itch that can't be scratched. Several times, Sarah finds herself outside the sleeping girl's room afraid that the bed may be empty, but the girl is always there where she is supposed to be.

When Safia walked into the ballroom she felt displaced by all the beauty, as if she were no longer on earth, but instead she felt as though she had walked into someone else's heaven. It even smelled heavenly. The delicate aroma of flowers hung in the air.

The Crystal Room had been decorated with opulent chandeliers floating in the sky and crystal snowflakes etched into the walls. Mirrors were strategically placed throughout the room to add to the magic and to give the illusion of space. The ceiling and columns were accented in a black that gleamed like marble, as if illuminated by the light of a million distant stars. The white seat covers were adorned with elegant black bows; arrangements of red and white roses graced each table and napkins alternating in black and white rested in each place setting. She felt like she had walked into a dream...Hinna's dream.

There was a silent electricity in the air as if anything could happen. If only her sister were here to see it. Safia shivered as goosebumps appeared on her arm.

Soon the guests arrived bringing Safia back down to earth, almost breaking the spell if they weren't all so beautiful as well. The men dressed in their dark suits with the twinkle from their tie pins, cufflinks, and watches catching the light. The women glittering in different shades of white, from evening gowns, to more traditional saris and langha outfits all accented with pearls or silver or crystal brocade. Safia could feel almost invisible in her slender off-white langha with silver blouse and matching stole covered in silver embroidery. Her hair was loose and threaded with silver. She was wearing a wide silver choker around her neck.

As Safia walked around making sure everything was in place she ran into countless cousins and aunties who were thrilled and slightly surprised to see her. That's what happens when you've been a hermit as long as she was. She looked over to her parents. They were seated at one of the more prominent tables smiling evenly...bravely, no doubt thinking of her sister as well.

Relatives stopped to talk and inquired politely about their health...about Laila.

Her mother had her hair pulled up into a bun. Her face was smooth and unlined but she still looked old, as if she had been carrying this load for a hundred years. Her grandmother was also there dressed in a white silk sari.

Safia went into the back room to see if Hinna had finished getting ready. She was wearing a langha of white and pink. The fabric was a tissue paper pink with rose and white colored embroidery. The fitted blouse had a heart shaped neckline and around her neck she wore an iridescent pink necklace with a sparkling pink rhinestone. When Hinna stepped into the ballroom, she was a vision. Clearly, a princess if there ever was one.

Hinna with her fiancé, Tariq, made a stunning couple. Tariq was over six feet—thank God Hinna was wearing three inch heels—with broad shoulders and a thick mane of hair. He had steely black eyes that were tempered by a generous smile and a deep, but gentle voice.

Now that most of the heavy lifting was done Safia could sit back at her parent's table with her grandmother and aunts and relax. Safia sat down just as the wait staff refilled the appetizers; there were skewers of lamb kebob, tandoori fish, and samosas filled with curried potatoes, alongside sweet and spicy chutneys. Safia loved the appetizers, filling up on these before they even got to the main course. All I need is this and cake, she thought.

"Why don't you go and mingle," said her mother. She was wearing a white silk sari with sequins.

"I'm happier sitting here eating," Safia answered, her mouth full of kebab. "Besides, I don't want to meet anyone."

"People will think you are anti-social."

"I am anti-social. I like it that way."

"Now…now…no arguing," said Safia's father. "I haven't said all my hellos. Why don't you accompany me and give an old man someone to lean on."

It was much more tolerable than Safia could have imagined as they drifted to different tables. Most of her father's friends gave her a polite nod. There was the occasional aunt that had imposed the big bear hug or the double cheek kiss. The music, popular Bollywood tunes, gave her something to concentrate on. And then, an odd thing happened. Inadvertently, Safia had begun to smile. They headed back to their table as Tariq's best man tapped the microphone indicating it was time to for speeches.

CHAPTER FIFTEEN

It has begun...

I can't deny I am excited. How I will enjoy this ball: the music, the dancing, I can even smell the food. My ears twitch to hear the latest gossip, familiar faces and new...oh, how I've missed you all. What I could tell you about everyone, the secrets that I hold like a key in the palm of my hand. Are they thinking of me on a night like this? While they enjoy the festivities, I am confined to a small, bland room and imprisoned in my own deteriorating body. My only consolation is that I know that he will be there. He will be there and he will see us.

If only it were me, I would shine like a Goddess. Oh, how I would own the room, but it's not me. It is her. There...I see her. Pretty, understated, and awkward, but still lovely nonetheless. She will have to do.

I miss going to parties, the fancier the better. It is not just about the dress, it is about the right dress...the one that brings out your inner power. In the right dress I can command the stage and trust me, the stage has been set—a chessboard it is. The pieces are white and black and my Queen is strong, but I will have her stay where she is for now. There are many pawns to play and of course, the old woman—*I have been waiting for you.*

He is here. I can feel him. All eyes are upon him. She won't miss him now. The game has begun. *All I need is a little music, and then...checkmate. Let the dance begin.*

Aidan arrived just as they were cutting the cake. He looked around for his parent's table. He found them easily. They were all there: his parents, his sister, Amina, and her husband, Kevan, and of course, Samar auntie.

His mother looked a little nervous. She drummed her fingers nervously on the table. His father put his hand over hers as a calming gesture. She looked at his father and smiled. He hoped her uneasiness was not because of him. Aidan had tried to call his family to tell them he would be working late, but his damned phone had died. He had taken his suit to work so that he could change at the office and here he was only an hour late.

His mother looked up and their eyes locked. Her mouth twitched just slightly and she had an amused glint in her eyes. Of course Aidan was turning every head in the room. He sat down at his parent's table and was enjoying the cake cutting ceremony, when he had the odd feeling that something was not right. Everyone was looking at him a little strangely. His father looked confused and his mother seemed to want to console him. Kevan was grinning. Finally, he whispered to Amina, "What's up?"

"It's your suit," she said. It probably should have dawned on him as soon as he entered the ballroom but he was the only one wearing a white suit. Well, the wait staff and he.

"The invitation said 'black and white'."

"Yes, but you're the only guy that would think to wear a white suit," she said stifling a laugh that made him feel eight years old.

"Wherever, did you get it?" she asked.

"Fish got it for me, said it would make an impression."

"Well, he got that right. On the up side, everyone will wonder who you are and their next question will be, is he single?"

Her smile was absolutely devilish as she said this. She had a very angular chin length bob that made her look like a flapper from the twenties. Her lips were painted a bright red and seemed much more garish on her pale complexion especially with her kohl black eye liner. Perhaps he would just sit here at the back and no one would notice him. All he had to do was make it to the buffet undetected, how hard could that be? While in line for the buffet, several people patted him on the back, "nice suit." Why was it that he was the only one that didn't get the memo? Aidan piled his plate high with food so that he would not have to get up again and then he planted himself at his table. Long after dinner was finished and dessert was served, and still Aidan remained there. Everyone else in his family was off schmoozing; some of the guests had trailed off to the dance floor.

Aidan hated to dance, yet he was putty in the hands of a precocious four-year old. A little girl in a white frock with big hair and long eyelashes had dragged him off to the dance floor where they were doing a variation of ring-around-the-rosie, which was fine by him…at least he had a reason to look dumb, but it was only the beginning. No sooner had she tired of him and a six-year-old grabbed his hand and he was back on the dance floor. Inadvertently, he had become the dance partner for anyone under twelve. A good thing too as the under twelve crowd was probably the least likely to be embarrassed by his dance moves. He was already a sight, he might as well let it all hang out, throw in a little John Travolta add a little James Brown and then smooth it out with a little Justin Timberlake.

"Who is that?" Safia whispered in Hinna's ear. She was watching a little girl being twirled around on the dance floor.

"He's dad's cousin's son, did well on Wall Street. I hear he's newly single…"

Safia wasn't finished taking him in when the music stopped and he looked up and caught her staring at him. He gave Safia a wink and extended a hand, inviting her onto the dance floor. Safia felt the heat rise up to her cheeks. The moment seemed to last forever and she felt both paralyzed and unable to turn away, that is, until Hinna shoved her onto the middle of the dance floor.

All she needed now was a slow song to make her more uncomfortable, but Safia was spared this awkwardness as the DJ cranked out more dance music. Safia, who generally didn't trust her arms and legs to move in alignment, started tentatively moving to the music and before she knew it, a strange thing began to happen; she started to have fun.

Safia had become at one with the music, letting it guide her and letting this stranger twirl her around. She looked around and Hinna and Tariq were taking down the dance floor. Abruptly, the music stopped. Safia was panting, beads of perspiration dripping down her forehead. There was a moment of quiet when she became very aware of the man that was standing in front of her, a stray lock clinging to his damp forehead, the smell of his cologne and strength in his eyes and for a brief second, she thought he might kiss her. That last thought alone was enough to induce a wave of ice cold anxiety. She was afraid she may have actually lost her voice.

"Thanks," she said to the stranger before her abruptly turning around and heading for her table. She dabbed her forehead with a napkin.

"That was great!" said Hinna. "He's super cute. Did you get his number?"

"What?"

"Don't you want to talk to him?"

Safia looked back to where she had left her dance partner, her vision was obstructed by people moving around the dance floor. When the crowd parted again, he was gone. Safia kept searching through the crowd. How could a man dressed in white simply disappear? Then something caught her eye — the twinkle of white, a fair-haired woman standing in a white sari that sparkled under the chandelier.

A strange, magical looking woman and Safia had no choice but to alter her direction. The woman had now become her goal and with it, a hint of panic that perhaps the woman would disappear the way a flash of light disappears in all but an instant. Whatever you do, you must not blink, Safia kept saying to herself. It felt like time had stood still as Safia maneuvered her way through people until she was merely an arm's length away. She could see the back of her head. Safia reached out and touched the woman on the shoulder. When the woman turned around Safia gasped. The light had played a trick on her. She knew exactly who this was. As the woman took a step away from the glare of the chandelier her features became older, more commonplace and her hair was really a soft white. She was someone Safia knew well and loved more than anyone.

"Safia, my child, let me look at you. How beautiful you look," said her grandmother.

Safia gave her grandmother a hug. "I thought you weren't coming today. You said you were too tired."

"I did but a little while ago I started to feel better and so I called your cousin Khalid and she brought me right over. Something told me I should be here tonight."

"I saw you in the light…you looked magical…ageless. Beautiful sari too. I don't think I've ever seen you wear it."

"This old thing. It's almost as ancient as I am. I had it stored away in the attic. Thank God for this good lighting making my old face a little more presentable, but I am still an old woman and this evening is taking its toll on me. Go see if you can find your father. See what time he wants to leave."

As Safia went off to find her family she was struck with an unshakable feeling. A feeling that she was being watched, that they all were.

It was the girl of his dreams or more accurately, the girl from his dreams that he was twirling around the dance floor. When he first saw her, he froze as if struck by lightning. He didn't know she was real. Instinctively he motioned for her to come forward, a flirtatious little gesture...a wink, and miraculously, she did. The crowd parted allowing her to move through but more importantly indicating that she did indeed have substance. She wasn't in his head and she wasn't a figment of his imagination. He wouldn't be dancing like an idiot with an invisible person.

When he took her hand it was small, delicate and soft but sturdy...real. This was no dream.

At first, he thought that he wouldn't be able to move but then an inner rhythm began to guide him. They moved a little awkwardly at first but then found their groove. Aidan wanted to say something but thank God dancing does not easily facilitate talking, and anyway he was afraid of what would come out of his mouth. How do you tell someone that you have been dancing with them for months inside your head?

The music abruptly stopped they were left facing each other. This was the moment when he should say something...ask her name, get her number, but instead he just stood there feet glued to the floor unable to express himself and unable to move. Then he heard someone call his name...damn. He turned around to address them and even managed a smile and a wave appearing halfway normal. When he turned around again, the girl from his dreams was gone, swallowed whole by waves of black and white spilling onto the dance floor as the music resumed.

Just like that the spell was broken. When he went back to the table his parents looked pleased. He had caught the eyes of many…but in a good way this time. Amina gave him a sardonic smile, "Break out some new moves today, Travolta?"

His mom looked as content as a well fed cat, did she know something he didn't?

There was only one person who had caught his eye. He wanted to ask, "Does anyone know who that girl in the white dress was?" Could he ask a more daft question at a black and white ball? At least Prince Charming had a slipper, what did he have? Not even a name…but he was a smart guy…he would find one.

Alan Memorial Hospital

There was something strange about the day. Sarah knew it from the instant she stepped foot into the hospital. It was an inkling that wouldn't go away until well past noon when she forced herself to take a deep breath. She felt better; the faint aroma of roses hanging in the air. It was almost like the faint residue of someone's perfume lingering in the background long after they had left. It was a nice smell and it was there no matter where she went.

All day long whenever she needed to catch her breath she would take a slow breath inward and their hanging in the background would be that comforting scent. She would think of it when she saw flowers being delivered to a patient's room or pass the gift shop in the lobby, any one of which could account for the lovely scent—but none did.

It was an itch she did not want to scratch, knew that she shouldn't scratch and so she let it hang like a question in the air until the next time she smelled roses. It wasn't long, in fact at certain times of the day and in certain parts of the floor the fragrance was slightly crisper. It occurred to her to follow the scent and it led her down a familiar hallway, sometimes it grew faint and she had thought she had lost it and was ready to turn away and then it would beckon her again.

She almost walked past room 7A, she had passed it several times during the day but had never noticed and never thought to go inside but now she decided it was time to slowly turn the doorknob. It was quiet inside — of course it would be. The sleeping girl is not likely to have the T.V. on. There was nothing unusual about the room; there was nothing hanging in the air. Sarah approached the bed and the girl lay peacefully and Sarah felt foolish for what she was about to do, but she did it anyways. She bent down and smelled her hair and there it was, the fragrant perfume of roses.

CHAPTER SIXTEEN

What a success.

I so love the scent of roses that I have decided to carry it with me. I have come so far. Yet, I am almost afraid to look down. I like it, this sensation of being over my head. It is so high up here, higher than I've ever been, higher than where birds venture to fly. I can peer at him through the window. I see him there with a glazed expression on his face. He doesn't know that I am here and neither does anybody else. How much fun I could have with this lot? It is no fun to be out here by myself. Perhaps I should just go inside.

I pass through the glass unscathed; my entrance into the room creates no more than a cursory ripple. Not a soul raises an eyebrow, nor a glance upwards, not even the involuntary shudder. They are so immersed in their dream and then I see him. I look him in the eye and I swear he can see me this time.

A shudder goes down my spine. I want to laugh…it's a first for me. I am getting stronger.

I see him loosening the knot of his tie and unbuttoning his collar. He is looking absently at his phone. I am brave enough to come closer to him than I've ever been. I notice the way his forehead furrows and how annoyed he looks. He is gritting his teeth. He wants to jump out the window. He wants to step onto the ledge and look down. I've always liked looking down. I've always liked roller coasters and the thrill to nearly falling to your death, the thrill of knowing that you are alive.

My heart beats a little faster. I'm about to do something I have never done before. I am about to take a leap. It's not something a shy girl would do—but then again, I've never been a shy girl. If he wants to jump, he will get his wish soon enough. It is now or never.

I take him by the hand and we fly.

The flowery scent of roses lets him know that she was there. Aidan felt a shiver go down his spine. It was the same tingle someone got when they expected a ghost to be outside their window. Even though you know you are asleep, it does not make a difference. He wanted to talk to her this time. This time he would not be so complacent, but even as he tried to speak, her soft finger shushed his lips. He expected her to be warm, but she was very cold like something not quite living. He felt the cold going down his body from his lips to his groin all the way to his toes, like a chilly electric current. He felt she was guiding him somewhere, pointing out a route. It was like looking at a map, only it wasn't a map.

Something told him not to look down. Look straight ahead and try to decipher her whispers.

"Don't look down." Is that his voice or hers? A forceful gust of wind changes all of this. Her hand slips from his and Aidan plunges straight down with exhilarating speed, like the steep drop of a roller coaster. He lands with a thud.

"Am I dead?" he asks out loud. He expects no answer. It is Fish who answers.

"Not yet, but you will be if you miss your meeting with Corbette."

"Where did you come from?" Aidan looks at the phone in his hand and wonders how he drummed up Fish's number.

"Just called you. You picked up the phone before it even had a chance to ring. Now, are you on board with the meeting?"

"No problem," says Aidan. "That's not today is it?" From the other side he could hear Fish groan.

Safia arrived at work feeling a little less burdened, calm almost giddy. She knew it would wear off. Stop acting like an idiot, she scolded herself. There was a lot of work to be done and not just the projects in her in-tray, there was Hinna's wedding as well. Safia was not sure how she ended up being Hinna's wedding planner but here she was mapping out venues and caterers and decorators. Hinna's emails came flying in at lightning speed—didn't she ever go to work? All morning she worked on Hinna's wedding and by the time lunch came she was famished.

"You look good for someone who's been up all night," said Orchid. She was wearing a tank top with a ballerina style skirt and looking extremely pixiesh. Leave it to Hinna to pick a Thursday night for her engagement party. They were having lunch at Mariposa Bakery her mouth full of a hearty tuna melt. Neal was looking almost conventional in khakis and a navy T-shirt, his biceps bulging out of his sleeves and revealing a dragon tattoo on his arm. He took another gulp of his protein shake.

"Maybe she met someone," said Neal with a sly smile.

"Maybe you should try eating real food," said Safia.

"Hey, no changing the topic," said Orchid.

"No, I didn't meet anyone," said Safia which was technically true. Safia was a horrible liar and both Neal and Orchid raised their eyebrow in unison giving her their bullshit look. Safia turned red and stammered with embarrassment. "A nice guy asked me to dance. That's it. I don't have a name. I don't have a phone number."

They both gave her a skeptical look but let it pass.

"Now do you want to see these killer pics that I got, or what?" Safia took the tablet out of her purse. Hinna's photographer had already sent her a ton of pictures to choose from.

"Pass them this way," Neal extended a hand. "Black and white, a girl after my own heart."

"Wow, everything looks so elegant," said Orchid. "You look great! Check out Hinna. She looks like she stepped out of a fairytale. You did a great job Safia. I'm going to get you to plan my wedding."

"Me too," said Neal.

"Hey, who's this guy?" asked Orchid. "He seems to be looking in your direction."

Safia took a second look at the picture. It was the guy from the party. Her cheeks began to flush. It did look like he was looking in her direction—across a crowded room.

"Is that the guy that literally swept you off your feet? Wow, he's hot. Find the guest list and track him down," said Orchid.

"Wait," said Neal. It looks like he's looking above you, at the ceiling. It looks like he's staring at a flash going off above your head. Check out the spec of light. It looks like a candle from one of the chandeliers may have gotten distorted."

Safia took a second look. She had never noticed this before. There was something unusual, glittery sparkling above her head.

The more Safia thought about it, the more it reminded her of sighting a ghost. A tingle went down her spine, and suddenly she knew exactly how to alter her concepts for the Jack Westland campaign. It was just the detail that the campaign needed.

Safia presented her concepts to Gavin, the account executive handling the Jack Westland campaign and of course Maya. Although they weren't as polished as she would have liked, they were pretty good. She could see Gavin smiling in agreement. Maya had a poker face, but as she sensed Gavin's approval, it softened to reveal her approval and eventual praise. The hint of an angel in the background had been just the right touch.

"Safia is one of our up and coming art directors. We expect great things from her," Maya had said.

There were only a few mild revisions and then they would be ready to present to the client. Safia let out her breath in relief as the meeting adjourned and she returned to her office.

"Tell me, do you believe in angels?" Gavin had said, mostly in jest.

Although it had meant to be a joke Safia stammered embarrassed. What did Safia believe in? She believed in the unknown. She believed something was watching her. Safia heard the ping of her cell phone indicating a text message. It was Hinna. "See you after work."

The streets were lined with shops, each showcasing beautifully decorated saris and langhas displayed in bright pinks, greens, reds, and sapphire and accented with ornate jewelry—gems glittering in every color. The only thing to distract from the beautiful window displays was the aroma of street food that hung in the air beckoning people towards grilled kebabs, samosas and chaat papri—a mélange of crackers, boiled potatoes, chilies, yogurt and tamarind chutney.

A sea of bodies reflecting the diversity of the Indian subcontinent flowed through the streets from modern teenagers in their stylish American clothes to women in brightly colored salwar kameez. The chatter of multiple languages hung in the air. Everyone seemed to have something to say. The streets were abuzz with the chatter of South Asian languages mixed with intermittent English, and often in the same sentence.

Safia wanted to stand still and take in the energy of the place—little pricks of electricity that made her come alive. Then something even better happened. It began to rain—juicy little droplets like mini water balloons splashed down on her forehead. Dozens of multi-colored umbrella's popped up. People ducked inside stores and restaurants, but Safia just stood still feeling the warm rain on her skin. When Hinna found her she was soaked.

"God, have you been waiting out here all this time? Where's your umbrella?"

Safia just laughed. It felt good. It had been a long time since she laughed a good deep laugh that came from her solar plexus. Hinna looked at her like she was crazy and then guided her to her favorite boutique. As soon as they stepped inside, the sales associates handed them a couple paper towels. It took a couple minutes for Safia to dry off.

Hinna had opted for a traditional Mughal inspired look for herself and the wedding party and although the design for Hinna's wedding dress had long been sent to the tailor, Safia still needed something to wear—something off the rack.

The store smelled like an amalgam of perfume and incense. Most of the clothing was elaborate and formal. They had outfits for the bridal party in heavy silks with ornate and contrasting patterns and long flowing skirts that grazed the floor when you walked. As always Safia felt overwhelmed. She pulled out one outfit and then tentatively another. Hinna on the other hand knew exactly what she was looking for. With the help of the sales associate she pulled out three or four outfits for Safia to try on. The rich colors of the first seemed to overpower her. They were too overwhelming, the embroidery too busy. It wouldn't do and neither would two others that Safia had picked out.

Next Safia tried on a dusty green langha with muted silver and white embroidery giving the outfit an old world feel. Safia stared at her reflection. A stranger looked back, someone more poised and elegant than Safia ever imagined herself. It was perfect. All it required was a couple minor alterations.

They couldn't leave Little India without a pit stop to their favorite restaurant, Punjabi Dhaba, for dinner. The place was one step above being a hole in the wall but always packed with people. By simply walking through the door the reason why became clear: the aroma of spiced meat and rich curries filled the air and roused their appetites. The warmth of the restaurant permeated through her body, from her fingers down to her toes. Safia found an open table while Hinna placed their order, and soon enough they found in front of them warm naan (flat bread), rich lamb curry and crispy tandoori chicken.

Now famished, an appetite long forgotten had emerged within Safia. She ate heartily taking huge chunks of naan to sop up the curry and licking her fingers. As Hinna ate, taking delicate bites and wiping her mouth with a napkin, she watched in amusement. Then finally tucking a loose strand of hair behind her ear she said, "Heard anything from the dream boat at the party?"

"He wasn't that good looking," said Safia turning red and trying to conceal her embarrassment with annoyance.

"He was adorable."

"Well, he didn't ask me for my number."

"That doesn't mean he didn't want it..."

"You're not going to do anything, are you?"

"Do I look like someone that meddles?" said Hinna trying to keep a straight face. It almost made Safia lose her appetite.

"OK, I'm done," said Safia giving way to her queeziness and they got the rest of their meal to go.

Alan Memorial Hospital

This is a place that is unusually cloudy and dreary, even when the sun shines down over the rest of the world. Typically, the hospital looms below an eternal shadow and so today is not like other days. It started merely as an isolated ray of light — a sunbeam that broke through the ever present clouds as if with intent and shone over the sleeping girl's bed, a halo to mark the sleeping beauty. Sarah was the first to notice it during her morning rounds.

It had been a late night and an inevitably early morning for Sarah, who was fueled by caffeine. Overcoming the aching of her bones, she went about with a vigor she did not feel. It wasn't until she reached the sleeping girl's room that she saw it, the ray of light…the halo almost as if a miracle was going to happen that day and in a way it did, and the girl was only the beginning. Soon beams of sunlight penetrated every single window, every nook and every cranny of the hospital as if searching for something.

Those patients who were always lethargic became more alert and those patients who never set foot outside decided to visit the gardens. Like a miracle, all those who lived and worked in the hospital whose disposition was ever grumpy, wore expressions that melted into a smile. Sarah thought, this would be the day. There could be no more perfect day for the sleeping girl to wake, for the old woman with the silver hair to stop her mourning and so Sarah waited...and waited.

But morning became noon and still the sleeping girl's room remained as silent as night. Noon turned into sunset and all the inhabitants were left to bask in the aftermath of a most unusual day. The sleeping girl lay without stirring, without blinking an eye or raising a finger, as quiet as the first day they brought her in—only her cheeks revealed the palest trace of color from where the sun had illuminated her face.

CHAPTER SEVENTEEN

I felt the sparks fly.

I felt them across a crowded room. He knew that I was there. I could feel his eyes searching for me. If there was any doubt, there is none now. He is the one that will set me free. The stage has been set, and what a stage it is. All of those beautiful people, all of those beautiful gowns and such an elaborate affair. I couldn't help listening.

He may not have wanted to come. Perhaps he even wondered why he was wasting his time, but I always knew he would. He can't help it. He is drawn to this place. It is his destiny, just like I am drawn to him. A white knight is what I see in a sea of dark horses. All these pieces on the board…which one shall I move first? Of course it is my Queen, my strongest piece that is most useful here —the one that will bring him nearer to me.

I move my Queen into his line of vision. The effect is undeniable. I have scored a win. I am elated, but I am not done. There are so many more pieces, so many more moves I can play. I am left to my cunning, to maneuver the pieces until he has found me. As he comes closer I become stronger.

The way the prophecy predicts, the way he is supposed to be. I can feel his lips upon mine. I am that close.

Aidan was accustomed to boardrooms. They were sober, professional, and conservatively decorated, but this one looked like it was designed by Disney, maybe that was going a little too far. It was painted with broad strokes of optimism. Someone had let their imagination go wild here. The phrase, somewhere over the rainbow suddenly came to mind. The room looked like it was designed for some west coast, right out of college start-up. The bright color just hit you in the face.

Aidan glanced at his partners. He was seated in between Fish and Jack, both seemed to get a kick out of the décor. Any minute now a seventeen year-old with in jeans and a T-shirt was going to come in and shake his hand, but when the door opened it was only the receptionist bringing them their drinks; coffee for himself and Fish and bottled water for Jack. Fish eyed the receptionist appraisingly. She had legs up to her neck and dead straight rust colored hair, if that was even a hair color. A minute later the agency came in. Aidan recognized Gavin, Maya…and her. His ears began to buzz as the introductions washed over him…it was her. Aidan consciously had to make sure that his mouth wasn't gaping open. Fish gave him a quizzical look but for the rest of the meeting he was able to hold it together while the agency gave their presentation.

Aidan tried not to be too obvious in the way he watched her, as if trying to solve a riddle. She was the mystery girl and yet she wasn't. They looked alike, that's for sure but her demeanor was softer, kinder and more sober. She wasn't exactly the temptress of his dreams, but no less attractive. He had to figure out a way of approaching her without sounding like a lunatic. The meeting ended on a high note and not without the customary exchange of business cards.

Aidan held Safia's business card in his hand. It felt like winning the lottery. He felt like he had deciphered a complicated puzzle. "Eureka!" he wanted to shout. It was only afterwards when he sat in his office with the door closed looking at that business card that he felt the little pricks of anxiety. What had started out as a dream had become all too real. Exactly what was he going to say? This was different than just asking out a typical girl. He did not want to sound like a moron. He did not want to come off as unstable and scare her away.

On the other hand, they were working together now and they had sort of met socially at the engagement party. He was still looking at his cell phone when there was a tap at the door. Right, he had almost forgotten about the meeting that was going to start in five minutes. He looked at the card again. His hands had become sweaty and he carefully put it back in his wallet.

Safia expected to be nervous in her first client presentations. She had attended these meetings before as a designer simply to observe and to answer questions. This

154

time as Art Director she was responsible for a large part of the presentation. She was expecting butterflies. What she wasn't expecting was the man of the hour. Boy would Hinna laugh when she heard this.

"It's fate," she could hear Hinna say. At first Safia felt mortified, as if suddenly realizing she was in her underwear, but no, she was fully dressed. No one she knew had ever seen her in this world that she had carefully crafted for herself. It did also give her the advantage of watching him in his world, his professionalism, his astuteness. She was worried her ideas might require some explaining…some convincing, but no, he got them right away.

Safia hoped to hell that she wasn't constantly looking in his direction. To detract from this, she focused on the other two clients. Jack Westland, whose persona was so magnetic that it was hard to look away, yet it made her weary looking at him too long…like gazing into the sun. Beside Jack was a more mysterious figure, Arthur Fishman. He was the proverbial wild card, the one that could not be pegged down…Rumpelstiltskin…the Joker.

It was surreal, like watching different versions of themselves in a parallel universe. Aidan had seemed so detached that she wondered if he recognized her at all. Of course his behavior was perfectly appropriate for a professional situation. What was she expecting…nudge, nudge…wink, wink, or for him to fall onto his knees and declare his love, as if she was some lost Cinderella. God she was losing it. She may even have to introduce herself again and remind him how they met. That would be humiliating.

She sat in her office holding his business card wondering if she could read anything into his words, "I look forward to working with you." She was still wondering this when her phone began to ring.

"This is Safia," she answered. The voice on the other end was unmistakable.

"You are an elusive one to get a hold of. I was almost afraid I would never get a hold of you. Would you like to meet?" he added.

CHAPTER EIGHTEEN

I am licking my lips…

He tastes so good. I couldn't help myself, I took a little nip and it was divine. Some think love is a walk in the park, but I know better. Love is carnal, and I can be quite insatiable. It was late and he had fallen asleep so peacefully when I came to him. Did you know he sleeps on his stomach, his face buried in his pillow? I ran feathered fingers through his hair down to the contours of his neck and then I couldn't contain myself.

I took a bite. Once I had sunk my teeth into him I knew that I could never let go. I thought I heard him yelp…how delicious. Now it is day and I watch him from afar, deliciousness oozing out of him. I know he craves it too, the salty, sweaty taste of flesh. I see it in the places he chooses to go…the company he chooses to keep.

When I look at her, it is almost like looking at a reflection, albeit one that is blurred and unclear but a distorted version of oneself. She thinks that he has come to see her. She is just a stand-in for the original. Enjoy your walk in the park dearest. Enjoy your meal, that smoky, spicy taste on your lips, the crunch of bread beneath your teeth and the look in his eyes when he is truly satisfied…because it is the most you will ever taste of him.

Deep breath in …deep breath out, for someone that was a hermit, Safia had taken a huge step. What am I doing? She kept thinking, why had she agreed so easily? Perhaps because he had sounded so affable on the phone and perhaps a small part of her wondered what he was like outside the dance floor…what kind of restaurant he would choose. Perhaps he would be a dud, a lemon and then she would tell him it was against agency policy to fraternize with clients, at least at her level.

When Safia got to the meeting place it wasn't what she expected. She could have sworn that he was all about fine dining, white table clothes, and meals that looked beautiful on your plate but left you longing for more. This wasn't the type of restaurant she was expecting. In fact, it wasn't even a restaurant; it was a food truck.

"It looks like a hole in the wall but the kati rolls (sandwiches) here are the best," Aidan said a little sheepishly. When he wasn't in the boardroom he had that boy next door quality about and Safia couldn't help but smile.

"No, this is great. I love fast food."

"Oh, this is so much more than fast food. Its gourmet food, served fast. It is a symphony in your mouth. Just watch."

"That's good, I should use that for my next campaign."

Safia watched as the vendor expertly created a sandwich composed of lamb marinated in Indian spices and melted cheese rolled up in Indian flat bread and garnished with mint yogurt dressing. It was almost erotic.

"Smells absolutely delicious," said Safia and then feeling a little mischievous added, "but I hate spicy food."

Her statement had the desired effect and the stunned expression on Aidan's face was the perfect mixture of surprise, confusion, and embarrassment. Safia felt like she had just kicked a puppy, albeit one with great hair and a deadly smile.

"Gotcha!" said Safia. "I love spicy food, but it was worth it to see that look on your face."

"I guess I walked into that one," said Aidan his grin spanning ear to ear.

"I would love a kati roll. Hmm…what should I get? I think I'll have the potato and egg kati roll with the cumin tamarind dressing. "

They took their lunch over to a vacant bench overlooking a little frog pond. An oasis in the city, thought Safia. Safia took a bite of her roll and it tasted divine. This guy was one pleasant surprise after another. Safia wanted to close her eyes and just savor the moment. When she opened them again his pale grey eyes looked at her with concern. She looked back into his eyes that reminded her of puddles after the rain and smiled to let him know she was doing alright. He finished chewing slowly before he spoke.

"I'm glad I ran into you. I was wondering if I would ever see you again...you know after the party."

Safia felt her cheeks burn.

"In this city you never run into the same person twice," he added.

"Unless you are attending the same wedding," said Safia. "I'm glad though...that I didn't have to wait that long."

"Must be fate," said Aidan giving her a devilish grin.

"Fate operating through Jack Westland," said Safia finally relaxing. "He's amazing. However did you find him?"

"You don't want to know. Part of me still thinks he's a quack, but I was impressed with your agency's campaign. I have to admit I have a lot of skepticism when it comes to Fish...I mean my business partner's ideas, but this seemed right on the money."

Aidan looked at Safia and smiled. It was so easy to be here with her. He wanted to hold her hand that's how right this felt. He found everything about her to be completely engaging, the way her soft black hair framed her face, the way someone could read every emotion in her eyes, the way she licked her lips when she ate.

She looked at him and smiled back, still savoring her sandwich. It was a smile that had nothing to do with him and everything to do with the way the right chutney can take egg and potatoes to a whole new level...that was probably most charming of all.

Aidan knew that look. Everyone that he had taken to this hole in the wall had quickly become an addict. In fact, he wouldn't trust anyone that didn't like this food.

"You like to eat, don't you?" Asked Aidan.

"Doesn't everybody?"

"You would be surprised at how many women pretend they don't."

"Oh, women love to eat alright. They just don't like to be seen pigging out. I guess I'm a disgrace to my sex."

Aidan laughed out loud.

"You're one in a million."

"You say that because you haven't seen our creative department," added Safia licking sauce from her lips, "you've only seen the suits. They're the face of the agency. If you could only see the studio…well, sometimes the most corporate idea comes from the most uncorporate looking people. That's why it helps to have management do the presentations."

"You'll have to give me a tour sometime. I'll probably look like a real stiff in there with all those hip, creative types."

Safia looked at Aidan in his single breasted navy suit accented by a maroon tie with the perfect windsor knot and black—probably prada—loafers. Hinna would be able to identify them on sight. The look did say banker to a tee but his awkward smile, the glint of amusement in his eyes and his choice of lunch cuisine said, don't judge a book by its cover.

"You're like some of our off the wall creatives. They're more conventional than they appear and I would say you are…more adventurous that you appear."

Aidan smiled, "that's the best thing anyone has said to me all day."

"This is the most delish lunch I've had in awhile, but I gotta get back to work."

"Let me walk you back."

"I wish I had time to take a nice leisurely stroll back, but I literally have to run to make my next meeting," said Safia getting up to leave.

Safia looked in his eyes and suddenly felt awkward. She wasn't sure if she should shake his hand or give him a hug; she had been out of the game that long. Yet, it was so easy to lose herself in his eyes, to fall into an ocean of gray that Safia wondered with a sigh what it would be like to kiss him, and for a second she felt herself melt. Embarrassed by her own thoughts Safia felt herself blushing hotly. She needed to stop swooning and say something.

"Hope we can do this again. I'll call you?" said Aidan grinning.

Could he read her mind? "Yeah, I think that would be great." She walked off abruptly before she had time to put her foot in her mouth.

Still feeling a little giddy, Safia had managed to keep her foot out of her mouth for most of the day, but now it was time to be coherent. She didn't feel like talking, so she concentrated on his eyes that were camouflaged by his thick spectacles. If only he would take those glasses off his deep blue eyes so she could better see his character.

He had that 1940s movie star look to him, gallant, seasoned, refined, and possibly brooding. She told him this and got the slightest hint of a smile. In the last few weeks she had made a number of progresses. It had been good day and she was just short of happy. She should have been happy. She wanted to be happy but there was always that nagging doubt that prevented her from giving into it. It was as if Laila was still holding the cards. Safia could feel her sister now looking over her shoulder, listening. Safia could almost hear her whisper.

I am always holding the cards, love.

Perhaps it was time to put her cards on the table. Until today she had never talked about the accident even though that was why she was here. Instead, Safia always talked around the accident. It was always about coping, coping with life after the accident, with life alone, and trying to be normal again, if that were even possible. Whenever someone said this to her, she wanted to say that she was never normal to begin with. It was, after all this time, that she finally admitted out loud in a voice that was barely even there.

"I was the one driving," Safia finally said.

She felt a shiver go down her back.

How long I have waited to hear you say that.

It was true. The two of them had been driving late one night when it happened. Something had punctured her tire. They had been bickering and Safia had lost control of the car. Only one of them had walked away. At least walked away with their body intact.

"It's alright, Safia. We all know it was an accident. You weren't drinking; you weren't doing drugs; you were just in the wrong place at the wrong time. You didn't see the debris on the road that punctured your tire. You need to forgive yourself for the accident."

"You don't understand. It was more complicated than that. We weren't like other sisters. She wasn't like other sisters."

I was never like anyone, darling.

"What do you mean? Many sisters are not close."

Therein was where the problem lay. How to explain what Laila was to other people? Laila knew exactly how to be someone's best friend. Safia knew what it was like to be stuck in her orb, trapped by her gravitational pull. She knew it, Hinna knew it, and anyone who had ever been friends with Laila knew. It was the swish of her hair, the batting of her eyes, and the honey in her voice that could always make a person give up their most prized possessions to her; clothes, jewelry, friends, even boys. Whatever Laila wanted she took—not this time, she didn't deserve him.

"Safia?" he said a little more gently, his voice bringing her back to the present.

"We were fighting about someone we knew…a boy."

I remember now. I barely had to bat an eyelash when he came running. Beauty is such a curse.

That is when Safia had to stop. She couldn't go on. Safia looked into his penetrating eyes, sure that he could read her thoughts.

"I can't talk about it anymore, at least not with you."

"I understand, but you should talk to someone. Maybe it's time you start talking to Laila again," he said.

"If only she could speak."

I am always speaking to you, if only you would listen.

It was true. It had been some time since Safia had gone to see her sister. In the beginning all she could do was sit by her bedside and cry, but as time went on, her visits became less and less frequent until she could not bear to look at her anymore. As she left the hospital, she felt like she was being followed, that her very thoughts were being breached. Even through closed eyes she could feel her sister pulling at her, accusing her.

She had spent a long time hiding. Perhaps it was time to visit Laila. She wasn't going anywhere.

That's what you think.

Perhaps this time she could make Laila listen. Listen she might, but would Laila forgive her?

Forgive you? I have bigger plans for you than forgiveness.

Alan Memorial Hospital

Sarah is at the nurses' station when something catches her eye. Something that she knows in her gut shouldn't be there. She decides to look around and she sees a man turning the corner. She's seen him here before, several times and always at night. He's going to room 7A; she's sure of it. He shouldn't be here, yet she is reluctant to stop him.

He's tall and attractive and his walk bears a certain amount of purpose, of authority. He looks like he belongs here. No one would easily confront him. Not wanting to be heard, she watches as he enters the sleeping girl's room. Ten minutes later, he comes out and surreptitiously leaves the hospital.

With a sense of urgency Sarah goes to room 7A. The girl is sleeping as peacefully as ever. How lovely she looks. That's probably it, isn't it? Some poor bloke who's fallen in love with a girl he will never be able to attain.

Shakespeare said that parting was sweet sorrow but he should have added something in there about anxiety. Safia had never really believed a man when he said he would call. It was such an all encompassing statement that could be used to either assure or dismiss someone. Call when? What did that mean exactly?

When Safia needed to forget something she went to The Dream House. It was 6 p.m. and the designers were either gearing up because they knew it was going to be a long night or winding down from a day of hard work. Orchid looked almost conservative in a kitschy sweater, skinny jeans, and ankle boots and Neal looked like the devil incarnate in tight black jeans and a black T-shirt.

He always had a grin for Safia that was always at the edge of being a smirk. "I wonder what he's like in bed," Hinna had once remarked upon meeting Neal. The memory triggered an embarrassed blush that crept across Safia's face and neck. Neal continued to smile at her as if he had just read her mind. Damn, why did Neal always make her think of sex. Perhaps because he makes everyone think of sex.

"Safia, are you done for the day? Join us for a game," said Orchid motioning towards the pool table.

"Why not," said Safia picking up a cue. She was terrible at pool so this would require all her concentration. The game can last much longer than anticipated when two terrible players face each other. When there was nothing else to catch-up on, Safia told them about her date with Aidan with as much dignity as she could muster.

"You sound like you have a crush," said Orchid.

"Nice to see you are not immune to the love drug," Neal added.

"You wanna ditch this place and go out for dinner?" asked Orchid.

"No, I think I will just go home."

Safia was at her apartment door and fishing for keys in her purse when she felt her phone vibrate. It was Aidan.

"Did, I catch you at a bad time?"

"No, I was just walking in the door. I'm glad you called. "

Their conversation lasted well into the night. Only when Safia's eyelids felt like they were made of lead and her speech began to slur that she reluctantly admitted to herself that it was time to hang-up.

"Before you go, when can I see you again?"

Their next lunch date was at a concert in the park. Safia was wearing a cotton skirt that was loose enough to allow her to a kick off her shoes and sit in the grass. Aidan, a little awkwardly, sat down beside her. They were away from the crowd, but still the sound of classical music floated in the air.

Safia closed her eyes and took a bite of her sandwich, taking in the low hum of the violins and then the delicate quick sounds of the flutes. She felt a soft breeze kiss her face. It was a perfect afternoon. She opened her eyes to see Aidan smiling at her.

"I hope you didn't think I was ignoring you," she asked a little embarrassed.

"No, I agree. If you really want to hear, you have to close your eyes. See the music in your head. In my opinion concerts should always be outdoors," Aidan leaned in a little. "Or even better, at night under the stars."

"Sounds so romantic...do you attend the symphony much?"

Aidan laughed. "Once or twice, maybe, but I have three years of piano, thanks to my mother. I think she was hoping I'd stick with it, but by the time I was in junior high I became kind of a bonehead, and didn't think it was cool to play anymore."

"Oh, that's too bad. Did you ever go back?"

"No, not to piano, but in college I fooled around with the sax when I wanted to burn off some steam."

The music continued to play in the background, but as more people arrived they were forced to make space, narrowing the gap between them. If Safia took a deep breath, she might get a whiff of Aidan's cologne and if the breeze were slightly stronger, Aidan may feel the tickle of her loose hair against his cheek.

"My dad loved jazz and he got me into it as well. Whenever I need to relax or unwind, totally forget about who I am, I put on Sinatra or Dean Martin and it takes me to a different time. A black and white movie plays inside my head. I can see the bandstand. I can hear Sinatra singing 'Strangers In The Night' while I glide across the dance floor with a handsome stranger. I sound like a freak, don't I?"

"You sound adorable. Besides I love freaks, they are my favorite people."

"That's great, because you have before you the Queen Freak herself in her idiosyncratic glory," she said tilting her head and in doing so, she realized how near he was and how much the distance between them had closed. If she tilted her head and came a little closer she could kiss him. She found the thought both desirable and unsettling. If Laila could see me now, she thought. She couldn't fathom how the thought had entered into her head but once lodged, it felt like a bucket of cold water thrown onto her from the sky and Safia physically began to shiver.

"Are you alright?" asked Aidan noticing the change in her.

"Ya, I just realized I'm running horribly late," said Safia looking at her wrist and realizing nothing was there. She stood up awkwardly and stumbled a bit, Aidan catching her by the elbow. He smiled at her hopefully.

"We'll get together soon…?"

"Yes," she said. "Absolutely," hoping he never let go of her arm, but he did and Safia shakily made her way back to her office. When she looked back, he was still standing there. She waved, but he seemed not to see her, instead focusing on something on the horizon.

CHAPTER NINTEEN

I am the chill in the air.

I am as fluid as water and as strong as ice. Of course, he senses an imposter. He may be looking at her, but it's me he sees.

Look closely, I whisper to him.

He has been destined for me and he will know it soon enough. She is merely a guide, a promise of more to come. She has set him on a path that will lead him into my arms. While she has him during the day, I visit him at night…and they have been long nights.

How time lingers in our dreams, and in our nightmares. I know too well. I have marked him.

It is a mark that is as delicate as a feathery kiss and as cutting as the fiercest bite. He is mine.

He craves me. Every time he looks at her, he craves me. He will find me. He will scale the walls that confine me.

He will break the spell that haunts me. I will awaken in his arms as I was meant to and both his days and his nights will be mine.

Only one of us can have him.

He felt bound to her like someone had sewn their hearts together and it felt good. There was no ball and chain, just connection. It was what he needed.

Aidan was casually flipping through Jack's book, "The Secret to the Universe; The Secret to You." He had come close to actually reading it. It wasn't that he had fallen for Jack but more that he was falling for Safia. Aidan felt happier and more relaxed than he had in a long time. She was the answer to a question he was too scared to ask.

Just like the proverb, you don't know what's missing in your life until you find it. He was wondering if his instincts were right about this, what else could they be right about? Problem was, his gut was saying this wasn't the whole story.

Something was wrong…Aidan was drawn to Safia. She was sweet, intelligent, and refreshing, but looking at her he felt there was a mystery to solve. Was she the girl visiting his dreams?

Now that he had gotten to know Safia better he understood, the two were not the same…in fact, they seemed like completely different entities. The girl in his dreams had a stronger presence…a rage even. As if she wanted to possess him, consume him the way no human could.

Aidan had to admit, he liked it. She was exciting and dangerous. Even when he was with Safia he could still feel her energy in the background. The air felt charged, like lightning before it strikes.

Absent-mindedly he answered the phone and within a few chipper sentences, his mother's radar went off.

"You're in a good mood. Is everything OK?"

No blood relative could keep a secret around her.

"Everything's fine Mom, the same…" Who was he trying to fool? "Actually, I ended up running into the girl from the engagement party. It looks like we'll be working together on the Jack Westland campaign. I think we'll end up friends."

"You and Safia?"

Damn it. How did she know her name?

"You've heard of her?"

"I've done a little asking around. Lovely girl by all accounts, but kind of introverted, a hermit actually. She went through a horrendous car accident awhile back. Are you sure you're interested in this girl?"

"I said we were friendly, that's all."

"Yes…Yes, I know what you said. Glad to see you so happy," and then stifling a laugh, she added, "Keep me posted on the wedding date…"

Aidan could just see his mother's mischievous little smile.

"What, with your psychic radar…there would be no getting around it."

Safia found herself humming, while at work, while on the train, a little melody she thought was in her head until she realized that she was humming it out loud. Everyone at work was giving her funny little glances and when she visited the studio Neal had even called her 'chipper'. He was not in a good mood and so it had been a backhanded compliment of sorts. It was new for Safia. She had always been pleasant, but never perky.

Aidan had called her late last night. Just hearing his voice could overwhelm her senses. Having someone's undivided attention after she had spent so many years trying to be invisible was blinding. It was like being caught in a headlight or being examined under a microscope, but she missed him when he wasn't there. He had asked her on the phone what she was doing on the weekend and without thinking she had said, "I'm going to a wedding show…wanna come? I have an extra ticket?"

Safia regretted it instantly. It was the first time in forever that Safia had asked someone out and if she hadn't been so out of the game for such a long time she might have been smoother.

It was a stupid question. Maybe it wasn't too late to take it back and suggest dinner.

"Or…if you want to take a rain check."

"Sure, I could drop by."

"Are you sure." Safia had to stifle a relieved laugh. "You are a brave guy. I was sure you'd be running for the hills."

"Hey, I have a sister and a mother and their friends were around all the time. I can handle a little estrogen. Besides, I want to get to know you more."

Safia could feel the blush creeping into her face and was glad Aidan couldn't sense her embarrassment.

"Alright, it's a date."

OMG, he must really like you, if he's willing to do to a wedding show with you. Even Tariq doesn't want to go and it's his wedding."

Hinna was sitting on her couch, legs tucked under her, wearing an oversized sweater over denim shorts. Her long hair was piled high on her head. She was definitely in work mode. A half eaten pizza lay on the table and Safia decided to pick-up another slice. Pizza was comfort food.

"Promise you won't tell anyone…about him."

Hinna eyed another slice and was mentally kicking herself for not choosing a healthier alternative for dinner.

"You've been starving yourself all week. One more slice won't hurt you."

"Hmmm…I guess I'll just have to work extra hard in pilates tomorrow morning," and then Hinna added a little more hesitantly. "She really did a number on you didn't she?"

Safia bit her lip. "She did a number on everyone. She did one on you."

"You could never be friends with her and escape unscathed," said Hinna

"Sometimes I feel like she's still there, in my head. Please don't tell anyone about Aidan. People gossip and I don't want him to know what a freak I am…not yet."

"You're not a freak. We were all under the same spell."

The long white corridor seemed endless. The floor was suspiciously empty. Safia could hear the click...click...click of her shoes, her footsteps announcing her arrival. The staff spoke to each other in hushed whispers. They looked at Safia suspiciously. People seemed to be whispering behind her back.

She was waiting for her. Safia could feel her presence getting stronger and stronger, with every step she wanted to turn around and run. It was too late. She knew. She knew that Safia was here.

There was her door, shut. The metal doorknob felt cold in her hand and the weight of the door was heavier that she might have imagined, as if it had been closed with the weight of a thousand years, but once Safia started to push, it opened quite easily.

The first thing she noticed was the fragrance of flowers. The room was lined with bouquets of beautiful flowers...or at least flowers that had been beautiful at one time. Now they hung dried and wilted in their vases, though still retaining their fragrance. It had to be her. Now Safia became very afraid. She did not want to come any closer, but her feet would not stop.

She looked at Laila's face – beautiful, serene, enchanted – in her rest. She felt overwhelmed with remorse, regret, and guilt.

"Oh, Laila," she said, tears in her eyes. As Safia's tears flowed onto her sister's face she began to move. Her eyes opened, clear...accusing. Safia let out a startled gasp as she bolted up.

"What are you doing!" she wanted to say, but Laila had already grabbed her hand. Her fingers tight around her wrists like steel clamps. Worst of all was her smile. It was drinking her in. Safia could feel herself wilting like the flowers, until she woke-up gasping in her own bed.

CHAPTER TWENTY

I walk amongst sleepers.

Such a busy place...so many dreamers. They walk right through me. I feel them like a tornado of emotions whirling around with no place to go. When I am near They feel me too. They feel a shiver up their spine...eyes upon them that they can't see.

They turn and look, but no one's there. So they clutch their purses a little closer, hug their sweaters a little tighter, then take a big sip from their coffee or tea hoping to drive away the chill, but I am not so easily driven away.

No matter, you do not need to fear for them. They have forgotten this moment almost as quickly as it has occurred. How fleeting their reality is. They think that it is just their imagination. I have simply wandered off to my next amusement. So many amusements, so many pranks...the possibilities are endless. I could spend all day, but that is not why I've come. Let me tell you a secret.

I've come for him. He is the only diversion that I need. He may not himself understand why he is here in this cesspool of bubble gum pink…how over the top, how tacky. As soon as he enters he will sense something different.

The air will grow thin and his heart will grow tight. Every molecule of my being will call out to him, reminding him of why he is here. He will feel my energy and he will remember the nights he thinks he has forgotten. All this will happen in a matter of moments.

Shhhh…don't breath. He will be here soon.

It was like grand central, as far as convention centers went it was vast, crowded, and endless in the number of stalls, samples, and wedding experts. Stall after stall of caterers, bridal fashions, astrologers, henna experts, makeup artists, and wedding invitations, all promising a perfectly blissful day…what happened next was anybody's guess.

Safia was here to check out decorators for banquet halls, who were adept at understanding all the details and intricacies of setting an elaborate stage. If there was any wedding that was going to be a production, it was Hinna's.

Aidan was running late and had texted her to go on ahead. He would catch up with her. Safia looked around at all the chaos, how will I find him in all this? she thought. Safia walked around, looked at the samples, and picked up brochures. There were a couple decorators that came highly recommended whom she wanted to check out. All around her were girls with their mothers, aunts, and sisters pouring over brochures, examining the embroidery in ornate wedding dresses and checking out lavish jewelry that would make any maharani green with envy. They were confident that they had found their princes and were on their way to their happily ever after. How could they be so sure?

An elderly woman gave Safia a knowing smile. She wanted to dispute the look in her eyes, to say, "I'm not here for me," but it would be pointless. Safia checked her phone again. Hinna was also running late. After about ten minutes Safia became nervous. What if he changed his mind? Safia took a deep breath and looked around the room. She was about to text Aidan to tell him that it was okay if he wanted to cancel, when someone caught her attention in the crowd.

Their eyes met and Safia knew he was coming towards her, valiantly crossing a sea of women in wedding induced comas. When Aidan was within shouting distance, she could see that the wall street warrior that he was had all but crumbled away, how lost and puppyish he looked amongst all the hubbub. Perhaps it was the air of looking ill at ease that made him appear so vulnerable and completely out of his element. When he smiled at Safia it was with an air of gratitude, although it was she that should have been grateful to him. When he smiled at her, it made her feel like she was the only person in the room. Suddenly every other person just disappeared.

"So why are we here again? Not that I don't love doilies and other lacey thing-a-ma bobs."

"I'm here to look at decor for Hinna's wedding. She's going for an old world Mogul theme. Hinna's here too but she's making herself scarce. Think of me as your official guide in wedding world and of course, help yourself to all the samples," said Safia grabbing two pieces of cake.

She gave one sample to Aidan who looked at it skeptically and then plopped the whole thing in his mouth…it was a big sample and he chomped appreciatively licking the icing on his lips.

"Sweet, light, and fluffy. I give it two thumbs up," said Aidan. "Now your turn," he added holding a sample up to Safia.

"You're not going to smash that in my face?"

"What type of person do you think I am? I Just didn't know when I would have another chance to feed you cake—big bite please?"

Safia took a bit of cake getting some on her nose. Yum, it was good.

"Now that we have our sugar rush, we should calm it down with some fried food." said Safia, looking towards a vendor with a tray of mini-samosas.

"Now you are talking my language. Fried foods are my biggest sin," said Aidan.

The samosas were filled with curried potatoes and peas but the dipping sauces were thin and watery.

"Hey look over there…drinks!" said Aidan. "Now I'm beginning to regret eating breakfast."

"Wait I still need to meet some vendors."

"Sorry, I got carried away," said Aidan.

"Give me another…twenty minutes and then we'll grab a coffee," said Safia

Seeing no line-up Safia made a beeline for the decorator that she was most interested in seeing. She showed them some of her sketches and grabbed their card. There were a couple others on her should talk to list, one proved promising and the other a dud.

"Alright, I've grabbed the crux of what I needed. I think we can grab a drink and sit for a while," she said pointing to an area where they were serving refreshments.

"What are you looking for in a decorator?" asked Aidan

"I dunno…someone that I can work with…someone that has the tools to understand and implement my ideas. Kinda like what I already do at work."

"You like doing this type of stuff, don't you?"

"Yup, I sketched out the decor for the engagement party."

"That was you…? That was amazing. No wonder you're at Corbette."

"Please, stop flattering me…"

"No, I'm serious and I'm not just saying that because I work with some of the most boring people in the world. Wall street just can't compare to your Dream House."

"Yeah, I do work with some of the most creative, complex, and flamboyant people you'll ever find."

"I think you have a gift," said Aidan.

"It's not just the work or the interesting people. Working at Corbette really saved me. It helped keep my head above water while my personal life was going down the drain."

Aidan looked over at the next table. A pretty girl, one who looked way too young to be getting married, showed off her ring. At another table there was couple of bored looking guys, with them was a twelve-year-old that was absorbed in a game on his phone. He looked at Safia. She was biting her lips. There was an anxious look in her eyes. There was something she wanted to tell him.

"I'm sorry to hear that, I mean about your personal life," said Aidan. Then after a pause. "Look at all these experts, they've really commercialized the whole process."

"You sound cynical. Do you not believe in weddings…? Or do you not believe in love?"

Aidan chewed his words carefully. He did not want to come off as jaded or someone with a lot of baggage.

"I was engaged once to someone I thought was the one. It didn't work out. She wasn't the one, but now I wonder if there is such a thing, and you…are you also recuperating from a disillusioned prince?"

"I've been too much of a hermit to find my Prince Charming. You could say I've locked myself up in a tower."

"Why would you want to deprive the world of someone as beautiful as yourself?"

"You think I'm beautiful," said Safia blushing.

"I think you are the most beautiful, kind, compassionate, and real person I've met in a long time."

"No one has ever said that to me before," and with some hesitation Safia added, "I lost someone close to me in an accident and afterwards it became hard to face myself. I'm sorry, it's complicated."

Would he still think she was beautiful if he knew the truth? Would Aidan still think she was beautiful if he could see Laila or would his feelings for her become as dim as a distant star? It was something she really wanted to know, but was terrified to find out.

"Please don't apologize. It's tough when someone you love passes away."

"The thing is she...she's still here."

A startled expression crossed Aidan's face and he suddenly looked paler.

"What...you mean like a ghost?"

"No, I wish. That would makes things easier. I would love to have a ghost around to talk too.

In many ways what's occurred is worse than death."

"Worse than death?"

"Yes, she's alive, but she's not with us."

"I don't understand."

"She went into the hospital and she never came out. She's in a coma."

Safia was in her office at work and for the first time, waiting for the day to end. She should have been working, instead she was chatting online with Hinna, who wanted all the details of her date at the bridal show.

Hinna: He's so hunky. If I weren't with Tariq you would have a run for your money. So tell me when are you going to see him again?

Safia: I don't know. Soon I think.

Hinna: No dinner invitations, no weekend getaways?

Safia: No, we're just hanging out...we haven't even had our first kiss.

Hinna: You're kidding. OMG Safia, you are moving way too slow.

Safia: You know what? I'm OK with it...and it looks like he is too.

Hinna: Hmmm...I bet he's a great kisser.

Safia blushed it had been a long time since she was kissed...really kissed. A kiss that started off delicately and then increased with urgency, a kiss whose heat she could feel pulsate down her body and awakening something she had buried a long time ago. Safia pinched herself. She needed to stop daydreaming.

Safia: I gotta get back to work Hinna.

With that message sent, Safia signed off.

It was past 6 p.m. and Safia was ready to go home. Or maybe a night on the town with whoever didn't feel like going home either. She knew Aidan would be working late. Safia was contemplating her evening, wondering what it would be like to live in the moment, not worrying about the future and the past. How liberating her life would be if she could just wipe away the past. Perhaps that's why she didn't hear her. It was a soft knock.

A tap on the door that was too light to be considered anything consequential. Don't evil witches arrive with more thunder. It was the type of tepid knock that couldn't possibly belong to Maya Lacasse, but as Safia looked over her shoulder there she was.

Maya was wearing a hip hugging leopard print skirt with a tank top that pushed up and emphasized her tremendous assets and a waist length blazer. Although she was not a large person, her presence seemed to take up the entire room. She sat on the sofa in Safia's office and smiled. It was not the type of smile that put Safia at ease.

"Safia, I was wondering if you had time to chat?"

"Yes, is everything ok."

Safia felt a nauseous, feeling a pit in her stomach. She was hoping that Maya's response would be put forth in some mundane detail.

"You know how happy we've been with your performance as Art Director. Gavin is pleased with the way the campaign is going and Blair is absolutely delighted with you."

"Umm...thanks Maya," Safia wondered when she was going to get to the but part.

"Yes, you have it in you to have a great career, especially here at Corbette," she paused as if searching for the right words. "I am not the type of person who interferes in someone's personal life. We let our staff handle their own affairs."

Safia wondered what she could have possibly done to offend Maya.

"However, we do have exceptions when an employee's conduct affects the image of our company or our relationship with clients."

"What do you mean?"

"Safia, you are a young beautiful girl. Many people are going to be interested in you, but you mustn't be tempted into having a relationship with a client."

"I'm not having a relationship...I mean we are just friends...friendly."

"Safia, I have been around a long time and I know the signs."

"Really, Maya there must have been some misunderstanding. There is nothing going on between myself and any client of Corbette."

"I hope you are telling me the truth because if you're not, it could cost you your job and you are a talented person Safia. I would hate to see you go," said Maya getting up to leave.

When Maya shut the door Safia realized that she had goosebumps on her arm. She was freezing; her neck and shoulders felt tight. She just hoped that there weren't beads of sweat going down her forehead during the conversation. God, she was a bad liar.

"You should quit," said Orchid. She was greedily holding a large drink in her small hands. Her hair looked a little wild. "You should totally tell her to screw off and quit. That's what I would do."

"Please, I need this job. I like this job." Safia looked around the lounge anxiously wondering how far Maya's eyes and ears extended. The sultry sound of jazz floated in the air. They were sitting at one of the marble top tables. Safia heard laughter and looked over at the leather sofa but she did not see anyone she knew. She was becoming paranoid. Neal arrived just as they were bringing a plate full of fried calamari and mussels with tomatoes, herbs, and garlic.

"How do you always manage to do that?" asked Orchid.

"Easy my appetite guides my footsteps," said Neal looking at the appetizers and then over at someone in the far end of the bar. He must have gotten a favorable response as he gave them a grin that was both sensuous and wicked.

"Careful, you might reveal your fangs," said Orchid. It was enough to bring Neal back.

"Looks like you're in deep shit," said Neal.

"How much did you hear?" asked Safia.

"Enough. You told her it was all bullshit…right?"

"I'm not sure she believed me."

"My advice is lay low until you're sure it's serious with this guy and if it is, then start looking for a new job."

"I thought every creative that left Corbette died an obscure death."

"True love always has a price."

CHAPTER TWENTY ONE

Should I feel guilty for being desirable?

Beauty is always misunderstood. Our perception of beauty is tainted by our fears and our desires. I have a chance now to right my wrongs, to gain back all that I have lost…or so the old woman keeps telling me.

It is not as though I have never felt regret. I feel regret every day. I regret the spinning of that damned wheel. My one consolation is that he is here now. He is so close. I feel him climbing through the thickets of my castle, ambushed by an unimaginable jungle—predators lurking in the distance.

He has not yet reached the entrance to the gate. Many tests await him. There are many distractions, but he will come. He longs for me the way I do him, no matter who he thinks he belongs to. He can't help but be drawn to me. He doesn't know what pulls him or what waits for him ahead—but I do.

It is the soft touch of my lips, the smooth caress of my skin, and the heat that burns inside me. I may be cold to the touch but deep inside me, I am slowly becoming warm. I am slowly becoming alive.

I feel the strength of the prophecy. It is his destiny that waits for him within these decrepit walls. It is a prophecy that has been foretold. The old woman has promised me this— and she will lead him right to it.

Aidan was sitting at a bar —that also functioned as an office—with Art and Jack Westland. They were discussing a sequel to his bestseller, "The Secret to the Universe; The Secret to You." Jack liked the title, "You Intensified." Jack was also interested in leading a meditation retreat. At least a thousand people had said they were interested.

"You should come along, Aidan," Jack had proposed.

Much to his surprise, Aidan was considering it. Perhaps Safia would enjoy it, maybe Jack was not as big a phony as he thought he was…nah, that was going too far. Aidan heard the familiar ping of his cell phone. It was his mother making sure he was going to be on time. He wasn't even sure he wanted to go.

"What's that?" Said Fish seeing Aidan looking distracted, "hot date tonight?"

"Nah, I have a family thing, just a bunch of boring relatives tonight…maybe I'll be late."

"You going to bring your girlfriend?"

"Umm…no…what…why do you think I have a girlfriend?"

Aidan felt sufficiently perturbed. If he was this transparent, what was he doing on Wall Street?

"Hey, don't start sweating all over your designer shirt. I know you, I can tell. You've lost that gloom and doom cloud that used to hang over your head, like some poor depressed prince. Personally, I'm thrilled. I miss the old Aidan, the one who believed he could conquer the world. The one that would go charging off into battle at a moment's notice. It's good for you, can't hurt business either. By the way anyone I know?"

"No one you know," said Aidan blushing hotly. He was about to say more when Jack cut in.

Aidan was never so happy to have Jack open his big mouth.

"I think it's great you're connecting with your family. You should try and make it home tonight, maybe even, umm bring your special friend."

"Thanks Jack, I may do that. As for any friend I wouldn't want to subject them to the old shark pit just yet."

Aidan dressed smartly. As he pulled up to his parent's driveway, he could tell from the motion in the window that the dinner party was in full swing. He looked at his phone. His last text was from his mother: *Don't be late*. He wasn't on time, but at least he wasn't late. His mother opened the door. She looked relieved to see him, but before she could say anything his niece came barreling into his arms.

"Mamoo, catch me," she said and then leaped into his arms.

Aidan caught her and swung her around. Shereen looked like her mother but had enough of her father to round her out. The effect was a sweeter, gentler more delicate version of Amina with an abundance of enthusiasm that children seem to possess. Aidan wished she could stay this way forever. She took him by the hand and led him inside. An array of guests were chatting and eating hors d'oeuvres. It was a familiar crowd, the same sort of faces he'd seen at any other dinner party. He saw Amina in the corner chatting with a young woman.

"Mama...looks who's here," Shereen said, running into Amina's arms. Suddenly, all eyes were on Aidan.

"There you are munchkin, and you've found your long lost uncle," she said giving her daughter a kiss. When Amina spoke the expression on her face became softer and her voice full of softness that Aidan found difficult to believe she possessed. At least it couldn't be said that she was a bad mother.

"I have dinner waiting for a little girl," said Asiya beckoning Shereen to come with her to the kitchen. "It's your favorite."

Lucky kid, his mother always fed kids dinner early and in the kitchen. Aidan dutifully said his hellos. Maybe it was his new found optimism but everyone seemed excited to see him. Samar auntie had changed her tone from disapproval to concern. He no longer felt like the black sheep. Just keep thinking the glass is half-full, he thought to himself. Even Amina smiled sweetly at him and refrained from the usual smart-ass remarks. Generally, she wasn't that nice, unless she needed a favor.

Feeling well, Aidan helped himself to some jumbo shrimp and chatted with a cousin of his. As it turned out she was doing her MBA part-time and so it was nice to talk shop with someone. Upon hearing their conversation his father had added, "Aidan is an expert in his field." Even his old man was touting his praises.

Dinner went by agreeably. He noticed he was sitting across from Amina and beside the new girl, what was her name...Nourine. Amina chatted pleasantly with both of them while Nourine kept smiling shyly at him.

Aidan was planning on ducking out early but the evening was not going as bad as he imagined. Coffee and dessert were starting to sound like a pleasant idea. He even started chatting with Nourine who worked in the actuarial sciences and was visiting from out west.

Being in his parents house brought back mixed memories. There were so many awkward years where he felt like a loser. Then when he got into Harvard his father finally started looking at him with a little respect. Even still, Aidan knew in the back of his mind that his father would have preferred MIT. He never said so, but Aidan could feel it there lurking in the background. Amina pretended not to be impressed but she stopped calling him, dumbass. Then when he had gotten engaged and brought home his fiancée his mom was over the moon. The best part was how much Amina had hated her. It still made him smile. Aidan looked up and there was his mom smiling at him nervously. Something was up.

He stayed around until everyone had said their goodbyes and the last guest had left. His mom didn't need help cleaning up; the cleaning service would be in tomorrow. Traditionally, Pakistani sons have never had to lift a finger; that is, unless they had a sister like Amina who would grab him by the ears and make him help her. Out of habit, and because Amina was still around, he began gathering dirty dishes and putting them into the dishwasher. His mom gave him an affectionate kiss. Amina gave him the evil eye, the way she always did when his mom singled him out.

It was late enough that he didn't feel like driving back to the city and early enough that he didn't want to turn in. Plus, he saw that his mom had put his niece to bed. Amina would pick her up in the morning so if he stuck around he might be able to take her to the zoo the next day. He missed hanging around kids.

Amina left a little later with her friend, but before she left she gave him the old nudge, nudge…wink, wink and asked if he enjoyed meeting Nourine. God, she was so obvious.

"She's fine, but she's totally not my type," frankly Amina would be the last person that would know his type. "Besides, I met someone else."

"Please, mom told me."

Amina looked like she had a lot more to say but his mom gave her one of her looks, and Aidan could literally see her chewing her words, rephrasing something that would've come out as harsh and judgmental. She was so like his father that it wasn't even funny.

"A nice normal girl is what you need, and Nourine likes you. She told me. That girl, that everyone saw you dancing with, sorry to tell you but she's a little out there, everyone knows it. In fact, you don't know what I've heard…"

"I don't want to know what you heard Amina, and I don't want to get into this," said Aidan hoping to put an end to the conversation, but Amina as usual had to have the last word.

"Suit yourself, but you don't know what you're getting into with that girl."

The building did not feel as ominous anymore. It was losing its hold over her. He was sitting in his chair with a preoccupied expression on his face. Safia smiled and it seemed to take the edge off, and at least his eyes smiled back. She was just beginning to realize what a frustrating patient she must be. Too bad, she hadn't realized it when she was being sullen, difficult, or temperamental.

She wondered what Laila would think of him. "I'd wrap him around my little finger," she could hear Laila say, as clearly as if she were in the room.

He was good looking enough that she would certainly want to give it a try. Safia looked at his right hand. It was poised with a ballpoint pen. A gold band fit snugly on her physician's ring finger…good for him. Safia liked to think he was with someone that made him happy.

And, for the first time Safia was seeing someone without worrying what her sister would think, whether she would hate him, or find him ridiculous and make fun of him endlessly, or if she would like him so much that she would want him for herself. Although Safia never realized it at the time, it was for this reason that she avoided going out with someone too good looking or too interesting; it was best not to tempt fate.

She told him this, saw him take notes.

"She doesn't sound like a nice person."

No, nice would be the exactly wrong word to describe Laila. No one became friends with Laila because she was a nice person. People wanted to be friends with her because she was magic. People and opportunity just opened up for

194

her—she was a walking lottery ticket, but it was also like being friends with a cobra. Her bite stung like fire and it could be lethal.

They had all lost admirers to Laila. It had happened to her and Hinna as well. Just thinking about it made Safia's eyes sting as if she were still in that car filled with smoke. As if they were still barreling down that road. She could sense the heat just beneath the surface. Hinna had been her best friend; how could she have done that to her?

When Safia looked up, he was staring at her. She was reminded of how deep and unending his eyes seemed, as if they contained lifetimes of knowledge.

"You're looking good these last couple sessions. Are you ready to go back to the night of the accident?"

"Yes, where we left off...I lost control of the car because we were arguing, but it was more than that. I lost control of my emotions. I lost control of myself," she was looking down at her lap; her knuckles were white as she tightly grasped her hands, now damp with sweat.

"Go on," he said.

She looked up at him and suddenly his eyes seemed much too feminine with long dark lashes that should rightfully belong on a woman, until that is, until stepping back and looking at his face in its entirety and then it all seemed to work.

"There was someone that I liked and I suspected she had stolen him from me. For several days, she seemed to be angling at something, something not good, like she had just one upped me. Everything was a competition with Laila. Well, by now I had become used to it. I learned never to like anyone too much because…well, if it was a choice between me and Laila, it was no contest."

"Did she steal your boyfriend?"

"No, it wasn't my boyfriend. It was someone else's. It was Tariq that she stole."

"The same Tariq that's marrying your cousin, Hinna?"

"The one and the same. They got back together after the accident."

"Why did it upset you that she broke them up?"

"I hated what she did to people…Hinna was her best friend. Sometimes she was beyond mean. She was just evil."

"Did you ever express your feeling to anyone?"

"No, everyone loved Laila. She was my parent's golden child."

"No one at all Safia?"

"Maybe just one…"

CHAPTER TWENTY TWO

Only the beautiful know my curse.

It is a suffering long misunderstood. I would not be here...imprisoned, if it were not for my beauty. They say beauty is only skin deep but this is not so. Another with my face, my hair, my skin would not be as beautiful.

It is in the fragrance of my skin and the music in my eyes and of course, the tone of my seduction. It makes my crime almost inevitable. People find it hard to ignore their desires. They bury their desires deep inside and punish others for their guilt.

They don't realize the truth, that if I have taken something that belonged to you, than it was never really yours to begin with—but that's not the way the world sees it.

Ah, there is my knight now. He grows more handsome everyday. How I long to look into those eyes, to run my fingers through his lush hair. I am watching him. Does he know I am there? Ah, and there she is...a poor replica. Can he tell a fake from a masterpiece? How understated...how bland she seems. How will she ever be able to retain his attention?

He won't need to wait long. I am almost there, almost able to reclaim my destiny. All I need is that one delectable kiss. I can picture it now soft, gentle, lingering…and as it lingers, it becomes more passionate, more demanding, more urgent until we are both on fire.

Aidan felt like he was about to scale a castle. The stone building covered in vines looked like a fortress, impenetrable but all it was, was a hospital. He didn't want to admit this to Safia but he knew this place. He had been here before. He understood too well why she hated coming here. He hated coming here, but Safia had looked so unsure, so vulnerable when she told him she hadn't seen her sister in months, that she was just getting up the courage go again, that only a jackass would not have made the offer, "Why don't we go together?"

He had said it, and before he could take it back, it was out of his mouth.

"You mean it?" she had said. She looked so happy. So relieved.

"Of course. If it helps you put your life back together, then absolutely."

It is a strange predicament coming to see this girl. Now he is wondering what he has agreed to. It was one thing to hang out and have fun, but coming here, this was entirely something else. This was serious. They had agreed to meet in the lobby, but Safia had texted him. She was running late another ten, maybe fifteen minutes. He had been hanging around the elevator awkwardly when someone asked if he needed help.

"I need to get to room 7A, but I'm just waiting for someone…"

"I know where that is. Let me take you straight up."

As the elevator ascends Aidan can feel the air getting thinner, or maybe he was just hyperventilating. He loosened his tie and looked at the orderly. The door opened and another five people got on. Now he was suffocating. By the time they reached the seventh floor, he and the orderly were the only ones left.

"This is it," he said to Aidan and smiled encouragingly.

Aidan stepped off the elevator awkwardly and watched the doors slide shut. His first impulse was to press the elevator button again and ride back down. That would be the smart thing to do. His hands are sweaty. It feels like he is wearing too many clothes. People walk by, and he avoids making eye contact. Ten then fifteen minutes pass by without an elevator arriving. Is it always this slow?

Aidan finds himself walking down a hallway. I should really wait for Safia, he thinks, but it is not his conscious mind that is directing his movement. At every moment his mind tells him to go back, yet something else entirely pushes him forward. He feels nervous…nervousness bordering on fear. He can feel his shoulders tense up. This part of the hospital is strangely deserted. When he finally reaches the room there is one last chance to turn away. Yet instead, he opens the door.

All roads have been leading to this moment. He sees that now. She has been here all this time waiting for him. She looks at him through her closed eyes. He can feel it. She is beautiful no doubt, more beautiful than he ever imagined. How red her lips, how smooth her skin. Aidan feels a pang of desire. He has the urge to hold her hand, to stroke her hair. He wonders what she must have been like when she was awake, what it would be like to walk with her, to hold her in his arms, to kiss her luscious lips and before he realizes it, he is bending over her bed, gathering her in his arms.

There is no future, no past…just this. This moment feels like the most important thing in the world, but something is not right. An alarm is going off. No, not an alarm…a ding. The high pitched sound breaks his trance and resonates for a few seconds. It is a text message from Safia.

He practically drops her on the bed. What am I doing? This is Safia's sister. He was about to take advantage of a girl in a coma. Has he lost his mind? Has he lost all sense of decorum? Quickly he rushes out of the room and back to the lobby where he and Safia had originally agreed to meet. As he sits down in an armchair, Safia walks through the door.

Outwardly, she is composed beyond reproach, every hair is in place and her makeup has been freshened. She is wearing a cashmere vest over a white blouse. Her dark pants are fitted enough to emphasize her slim figure and her high heels emphasize her long legs. She tells herself she's dressed-up for Aidan, which is partially true. A paragon of professionalism, she looks like she's just come out of a meeting, which is technically true, as she'd been at a client meeting that was running late, but looking a little closer, the weariness in her eyes became apparent and that her mouth has been composed into a firm line of determination. Her posture is a little tense and her enthusiasm forced. When she sees Aidan, she gives him a smile that she really doesn't mean.

He smiles back uneasily and Safia realizes what a mistake it was to ask him to be here for her. This is more than she's ever asked of anyone. She's touched that he is here for her but this is not where she wants to be. What she really wants to do is turn around, run back to her apartment, and bury herself in hot tea, dark chocolate, and her latest designs. Aidan stands-up and Safia walks over to him and gives him a hug burying her face in his chest. It's a first for her to be able to reach out to someone this way. Somehow, Aidan senses this. His embrace is warm and reassuring. He's come all this way for her, and somehow it solidifies this all that much more. There is no turning back now.

Aidan drinks her in. Her hair is silky. Her body feels so soft against his. God, she smells good. She's trembling in his arms and for the first time he realizes how scared shitless she is.

"Hey, it's going to be fine. I'm here for you," says Aidan.

When she looks up at him, her mascara is smudged and there is a tremor in her bottom lip. She looks like a scared little kitten.

"I'm so glad that you are here, but I think I need to go up by myself," says Safia.

"Are you sure? I'm right here if you need me."

Safia nods uncertainly. One thing she know for sure, this is something she needs to face alone. She presses the elevator button and it opens seconds later. She steps in and puts on a brave face as the doors slide shut.

She notices the activity around her as she walks out of the elevator. The staff chatting at the nurses' station, a patient in a wheelchair being guided down the hall. It all looked so normal, so everyday. Life goes on and it has been going on all around her as she has buried herself in guilt and despair. Finally, she reaches Laila's room. She stands for a moment with her hand flat against the door before she opens it. There she is.

Safia walks over to the bed. Her hair has gotten longer. How pretty the dark tresses look against her pale skin. She looks so peaceful as if she's merely asleep. Safia runs her fingers through Laila's hair. It's too much to be here with her like this to know that she may never get up again. It isn't fair. Laila had so much to live for. Safia can't stop the tears rolling down her cheeks but it's only the beginning. It's not enough to simply shed tears, Safia's body convulses in sobs. There is a part of her that needs to let out a deep guttural howl. She understands now why people beat their chests and pull their hair out with grief. There has been a storm brewing inside her for way too long. Like all storms it will not be satisfied until it's run its course.

When it is over...when it is finally over, she looks like hell. Her perfect hair looks wild and untamed. Her face smeared with make-up and her clothes disheveled and wrinkled, but it's out. It's all out. Before she leaves, Safia make a promise that she will never abandon her sister again. She will be here for her, as long as it takes.

Alan Memorial Hospital

When Sarah begins her evening shift, she knows something has happened during the day. People walk quietly past room 7A.

"A relative was here today," someone tells her, motioning towards the sleeping girl's room. "She had a melt down. It wasn't pretty. She had to be given a sedative and escorted home," they add. Sarah nods her head soberly. Of course it is a tragedy but there is something else that gnaws at her. It is the awareness that the girl belongs to someone else, a family. For a time she had forgotten this, the way to forget anything that becomes a fixture in one's life. For too many years she's simply been their princess, something novel and mysterious like a talisman or a good luck charm.

The next time Sarah walks past room 7A she has the urge to put her ear to the door. It's a silly thing to do. She can just go in if she wants. She tries to turn the door knob but it is stuck. She tries to push the door open but it won't budge. She puts her ear to the door and she can almost feel it vibrate. It is like listening to the ocean, a low moaning swoosh — sad and melancholy and so full of sorrow. It frightens Sarah. She is pushing hard to unjam the door and suddenly it flies open and with it, a gust of wind rushes out. Sarah stands for a moment taking in the quiet.

She walks over to the girl. All is well. There is nothing to be concerned about. Sarah moves her hair out of her face. There much better…on her cheek is but a single tear drop.

CHAPTER TWENTY THREE

I have no words to express my anguish.

He has slipped through my fingers. There is nothing left in me, but sorrow. Yet he was here, I was in his arms. There was no denying the passion that he felt. I could feel the beating of his heart calling out to me and my body responding, every molecule within me energized. I could hear the swoosh of blood running through my veins, the cold in my limbs being replaced by a distant heat. The warmth of being held by him permeates my body.

Fate has played a trick on me. As harsh as any winter frost, it has all turned to ice, just moments before his lips grazed mine, moments before our eyes locked. There is no one left with me, except her. My tears flow through her and my sorrow permeates her body. How I want to reach out to her. She is still my only hope. How brave she is, how brave she has always been.

When we have cried all the tears we have left to cry, as long as she is strong I have not lost hope. I will not lose this battle with destiny. He has come to me once. I have seen it with my own eyes.

He will come to me again.

The world has been painted in different shades of yellow, and each guest shined like the sun. Of all the wedding ceremonies, Safia loves the mehndi the best. Safia is wearing a silky, honey yellow salwar kameez (tunic); her hair has been pinned half up with tresses pulled out around her face and some light make-up that completes her look.

Rosina auntie, Hinna's mother, greets Safia at the door and gives her a huge hug. It's the type of embrace given to a long lost relative and until now Safia hasn't realized what her seclusion had done to the rest of the family. Safia can feel the tears welling up in her eyes.

"I'm so happy that you're here," she says wiping her eyes, "and what a help you've been. Hinna would have been lost without you."

This is true. Hinna has a reputation for going off on a tangent.

"She's been great to me too. She's gotten me out of the mountain of work I've buried myself into by giving me more work, but it's been fun. More fun than I have had in a long time."

"When your time comes, don't let her off easy," says Rosina with a wink.

"I wouldn't think of it," says Safia.

"Hinna is upstairs in her room. She'll need help getting ready."

Safia knocked on Hinna's door and then entered quietly. Hinna was already dressed but there were two girls there presumably to help her with her hair and make-up. She gets up to give Safia a hug. The outfit she's wearing is a pale, baby chick yellow with a lot of intricate stitching and embroidery that wasn't noticeable until she came closer. It really is subtle and classy not the type of thing she would have predicted Hinna would choose. Hinna seems to have read her thoughts.

"I'm stealing your style. I'm going for understated elegance."

"You're too beautiful to ever look understated," said Safia, "Your langha is gorgeous and so intricate."

"I know. My mom picked it out; it's the only thing we agree on. I need to get my hair and make-up done now. I'm wearing my hair down, school-girl style even; my make-up will be au naturale, so it'll take a while. I'm keeping the whole event intimate and traditional—just us girls."

"How many people are coming?"

"About fifty, mmmm...what's that smell? I think my Mom has set out the appetizers. "

"You can smell that from here?"

"I haven't eaten all day."

"Enough said. Let me see what I can grab."

Safia headed down the stairs and towards the kitchen. More guests arrived, aunts, uncles, and cousins she hasn't seen in ages. They all give Safia surprised smiles. She sees her grandmother sitting on a chair in the corner. Her eyesight is weak and it's not until she gets close that her grandmother recognizes her. She kisses her grandmother hello. This is the most she's seen her grandmother leave the house in years.

She looks around for her mother, who is chatting with someone she doesn't recognize. Upon seeing her, Safia's mother motions for her to come over. Then Safia realizes who this woman is; its Tariq's mother, Zara. She can see the resemblance now. Safia says hello.

"So this is the girl that is responsible for the beautiful engagement party." They've met several times but this is the first time she'd really looked at Safia. She sees what everyone else sees, a normal, young woman. Her mother goes on a bit more about her accomplishments. Safia knows where this is going. Her mother is setting her up as someone eligible. She doesn't know about Aidan yet, thank God. She can see that a buffet has been set up in the dining room.

"I promised Hinna some food. She's starving. I better get a move-on before the buffet gets crowded."

"Yes…yes, mustn't keep the bride waiting," says Zara auntie.

As Safia walks over to the dining table more guests have arrived. The house is abuzz with activity, traditional music plays in the background and beautifully dressed children run throughout the place. They swarm past her towards an unknown destination. Safia gets to the buffet. Hinna's mom has gone all out and these are only the appetizers. Safia grabs not one plate but two and starts helping herself to samosas, tandooried chicken pieces, vegetable pakoras, and even some skewered lamb. Well, that's enough spicy and now for the sweet. She adds fruit salad, cupcakes, and cookies.

When Safia gets back to Hinna's room it's like a slumber party. It is full of young cousins in high school, talking about what they want to wear to prom and friends…friends from college, friends from work, friends from every corner of the world all laughing and giggling and going over Hinna's outfit, her make-up, and her jewelry. Hinna has chosen emerald green bangles to compliment her pale langha. Her hair has been done already; loose curls pinned away from her face and flowing down her back. The beautician is putting the finishing touches on her make-up, which looks fresh and mild with light colors. She looks like a spring angel.

As Safia enters the room carrying trays of food, all attention falls on her and she is temporarily the star. She sets the food down near Hinna.

"Oh my God, you're a saint," she says. Then adds, "at this rate I'll never have to leave."

All eyes turn to Safia and suddenly recognition dawns on the other guests. They know who she is. Safia wishes she could disappear but then the moment is gone and Safia finds herself amongst hugs and pecks on the cheek and comments such as, "I haven't seen you in ages...how have you been?" Everyone is in party mode so these questions are easy to deflect.

Safia looks over at Hinna, who is simultaneously showing off pictures of the engagement to one friend while conversing with another, all the while stuffing her face with food. At this rate she'll ruin her make-up before they take her downstairs.

There is a knock on the door and Hinna's mom pops in. The henna artist and most of the guests have arrived. It is time to bring Hinna down to the party.

"Five minutes," says Hinna. "I just need to finish this cupcake."

When Hinna is done, they bring her down. The six of them are holding a red dupatta (long piece of cloth) above her head. The procession moves slowly down the stairs and into the basement where the party will take place. As they enter everyone is singing wedding songs, the same traditional songs that have been sung for generations. They sit Hinna down in a cushioned area that has been set aside for her. There are two henna artists at the party, one to decorate Hinna's hands and feet and the second for any guests that wants to get their henna done.

The henna artist has come with icing cones filled with henna and she starts an intricate henna design on Hinna's hands. The bride's side of the family and the groom's side sit opposite each other, each singing their respective songs. Someone in the middle is playing a tabla (traditional drum) that will provide a beat to their songs. It's traditional for the songs at times to poke a little fun at each other. When one side attempts to do this, the other side will hiss and boo to try and ruin their song.

It is difficult for Safia not to be seduced by the cheeriness of the party, to partake in the camaraderie of the women, to sing at the top of her lungs, and to boo even louder. She wishes Aidan could see her enjoying herself with such abandon.

It is 11 p.m. and Aidan is sitting in his car. The parking lot is near deserted. What had provoked him to come here? He kept telling himself that he was just going to drive around, maybe grab a burger...but he knew better. The minute he stepped into his car, he knew that he would end up here. He is momentarily distracted from his thoughts by the burger and fries sitting on his passenger side. He dips his hand into the bag and grabs some greasy fries and shoves them into his mouth. They are becoming soft, losing their crispness. Aidan is not fazed by this, he's staring at the building as if he were watching a movie.

It is an old non-descript building except for the bright "H" on the roof. At night it looks fairly ominous — more like a prison than a hospital. Ever since he had seen the sleeping girl, he had wanted to come back. It wasn't even a choice anymore, something else was driving him now. Many times he had driven by the building not daring to go in. Today he had ventured as far as the parking lot. Visiting hours were long over, but he might still be able to sneak in.

The idea filled him with excitement and panic, being in the same room with her again. There is something about this situation, about her that's not right. She's more than an innocent girl lying in a hospital bed. He doesn't want to admit this but on some level he knows it's true. Every time he thinks he has his head on straight, it goes back to her. What would Safia do if she knew he was sitting here like this?

He needs to stop thinking about this place…perhaps if I just go inside. No, he can't give in to this insanity. He realizes that he has been sitting here for thirty minutes. He has to make a decision. He's afraid of what might happen if he goes into the hospital. He's afraid of her. He starts his car and drives away, still he can almost feel her staring at him following him with invisible eyes. He keeps glancing in his rearview mirror. He strains against the silence of the night for any kind of sound. This is the last time, he tells himself even though he knows it's not true.

Safia is licking her fingers when someone taps her on the shoulder. She has just polished off a full plate of food. Maha, Hinna's younger sister asks if she wants to have her henna done. Maha is in junior high — the age when she wants to look older than she actually is. She's wearing a little too much make-up and her frock is a little too tight at the bust but she still looks lovely.

"Sure," says Safia. Now that she's finished dinner, the timing is perfect. The second henna artist is a young girl who looks like she should be in college.

"How old are you?" Safia wants to ask but is too polite and for a second she's worried that the design might be clunky and amateurish.

"Just do my palm," says Safia. "I have work tomorrow."

The henna artist starts with some very fine lines and within minutes a shape begins to emerge. It is a beautiful flower, something one might see on a Persian Rug. Ten minutes later she's putting the finishing touches on the petals.

"Thanks," says Safia, "this is gorgeous."

Safia looks over toward Hinna. It looks like her henna is done. She's dying to take a look. The design on Hinna's hands and feet is extremely delicate and intricate, a beautiful mosaic of flowers spinning out of flowers and vines running from her palm to her fingers. Against Hinna's fair skin the contrast is striking, tomorrow if they were lucky the color of the Henna will turn a deep red, but black henna has always been especially beautiful to Safia. Hinna is momentarily alone as someone has gone to get her some dessert. She looks tired but in good spirits.

"How are you doing? Have enough to eat?" the usual questions.

"I'm good. Are you sure you're not tired?"

"I am but it's a good tired. You know I never thought this day would come."

Without anything more being said Safia understands what she means.

"I went to see her, you know."

"You did...? How was it?"

"Hard...but I needed it. It was time. I almost feel like she is here with us."

"Trust me, if she were here this day would not be happening," Hinna's voice carried an edge that was hard to ignore. "I know that this is wrong, but I'm glad she's not here...not today. You're lucky too that she's not here to mess things up with you and Aidan."

Safia's mouth is dry. She doesn't know how to respond. This is more than Hinna has ever confessed before, and here she was thinking everything just rolled off Hinna without leaving any kind of imprint. Safia was saved from the pain of an awkward silence as someone brought over a bowl of dessert for Hinna, warm gulab jamun (dumplings soaked in rose flavored syrup) with vanilla ice cream—East meets West.

Safia is in luck as Maha hands her a bowl of dessert just as the music starts.

"Be careful of your mehndi," she says.

Safia must find a creative way to hold the bowl and eat with one hand, but it's worth it. The gulab jamuns are delicious, warm and soft and syrupy. Guests have cleared the center of the room in anticipation of the performances. Young girls in brightly colored outfits twirl to Bollywood favorites. Some are exceptionally good and others are just having good fun. Safia wishes she had the guts to be so uninhibited. So free. She is clapping and cheering for the girls when she notices someone; straight dark hair cut below the chin and garish lipstick.

She seems to be eyeing Safia carefully but doesn't respond when Safia smiles at her. Safia is fine with being ignored but when the music temporarily stops the woman decides to strike up a conversation with her. Her voice conveys a friendliness that isn't really there.

"Great party, isn't it? I don't think we've met. I'm Amina."

Of course, now Safia recognized her, she was Aidan's sister.

"It's great to meet you. I'm Safia."

"I know…" she said leaving a very long pause. "I saw you at the engagement party. You're quite a dancer. You should be up there."

"Naw, I think I just found the right partner."

"Well yes, that too, but dance partners can be finicky as the music changes. We mustn't get attached."

"I don't think I know what you mean."

"I think you do," says Amina.

Safia was taken aback by the comment, but by that time the music started again and another group of girls in bright clothes took center stage, Amina slipped into the shadows of the room.

CHAPTER TWENTY FOUR

I knew he'd come again.

I can feel each step…each stride…each breath. I can feel his gaze through the walls that separate us. We are linked now, bonded by an invisible cord and all I need do is give it a little tug. He will feel me calling. I have infested his head, his heart…his manhood.

You see, every time he leaves. He takes me with him, not all of me but just enough. I am there always, hovering over him. I am closer to him than his own shadow.

He feels torn. He thinks he loves someone else but she is no match for me. She is no match for him. I am the one he is waiting for. Do not fight so hard, I want to say. Come to me.

Let me possess you. Like a second skin so that I may permeate through your armor and obliterate your defenses. I am the only shield that you will ever need. Let me inside you. Let me see through your eyes and let me guide your steps. Let me whisper in your ear and let that whisper trickle down to your heart and find its home in the deepest part you.

For that is where I belong.

He had tried to be zen about his life. He had even taken his mother to one of Jack Westland's meditation sessions. His mother had always been about finding a higher calling. It was held in a clearing in a beautiful arboretum. His mother had been thrilled to accompany him with her copy of Jack's book in tow and so had another fifty of Jack's dedicated disciples. After speaking briefly, Jack had led a meditation session.

It had been so peaceful, almost monastic. Aidan could feel the breeze lightly graze his face. He could hear the rustling of leaves. He was quiet and yet he was intensely aware of everything even as all his problems and baggage buzzed around him like a hornet's nest. He was detached. He could step away from it and watch it dissolve. Suddenly, he felt lighter and the top of his head began to tingle. Aidan was beginning to think that Jack had stumbled onto something, either that or they had put something in the coconut water.

Unfortunately, Aidan wasn't able to stay for the entire retreat but if the rest of the guests got as much out of it as he did, this was going to end up a gold mine. Aidan was still feeling a little high, a little other worldly when he got what looked like a benign piece of mail. Holy shit, it pierced him right in the gut and Aidan could feel all his enlightenment evaporating. There was no denying it, she had him right where she wanted him. Aidan could feel his pulse race and his heart skip a beat. Maya LaCasse was killing him.

He had opened what was to be the first invoice from Corbette advertising. He felt the twisting of the knife, the amount was way more than he had anticipated and they hadn't even finished with the campaign. She was really giving it to them.

"Have you seen this?" he asked Fish.

Fish took a quick glance and then raised an eyebrow, which was saying a lot for Fish. It was his, I want to look calm but I'm a little shocked, look.

"Who knew revisions could cost so much?" he said.

"Did you say anything to her? Because I'm wondering how, 'we're on a budget,' has been interpreted as 'we're made of money?'"

Fish looked suspiciously guilty.

"I have half a mind to call their billing department. Maybe we should switch agencies?"

"Let it go," said Fish shrugging it off. "We're still way in the black. Jesus, you think this is bad, you should see how lawyers bill."

Aidan wondered if Fish might be a little impressed by Maya's gall.

"What are you not telling me?" asked Aidan a little worried.

"I just mean, better the devil you know, than the devil you don't know," replied Fish.

"Trust me, this is one devil you don't want to know any better. Maya LaCasse could run circles around us."

Fish did not look convinced but Aidan did not have time for a discussion. He looked at his phone…still no response from Safia.

It was starting to feel like she was walking a tightrope. There was an uneasy feeling in the pit of her stomach that she might lose her balance. Safia stared at her phone as if in doing so a solution might magically appear. There was another message from Aidan. Guiltily, she responded that she was too busy for lunch. This would work for a little while but she was running out of evasive maneuvers. She even thought about seeing her shrink. It would be the first time she had initiated a meeting. She needed to talk to someone but she didn't know what to say.

Then again, perhaps she was wrong. Perhaps she hadn't understood properly what she had seen, but in her mind there was no other way to interpret it. It felt like a darkness looming overhead. Safia didn't believe in curses…or the evil eye but something was there. Something was very wrong.

The point in time where everything seemed to go awry was at Hinna's mehndi. Everything was fine between them, great even and then it all changed. That's when the voice nagging at the back of her mind first appeared. It was probably that voice that had led her on a path that she may have written off before. It happened no less than a week after the mehndi. It's the type of thing a person knows and may regret, but does anyway because it's who you are and no shrink is going to change that.

Safia had fallen asleep in front of the television in the most cliché sort of way — remote in her hand, greasy potato chip crumbs lining her mouth, her flannel pajamas a testament to the sexless night ahead. She had been staying up waiting for Aidan to call…another sorry cliché. He had either forgotten or she had slept through it. For two hours she lay dead to the world until she heard someone calling her. That's when she awoke. Someone had called her name with determination, urgency even.

Against her better judgment Safia woke-up. She knew that voice, she knew that tone and it could only belong to one person. She also knew it was a bad idea. Perhaps some of us are just destined to sabotage our own happiness. It can't be helped.

The whole time Safia kept trying to make deals with fate. I'll just put on my coat and go down stairs, and if there's no cab I'll turn around. But there was a cab as if it had been waiting for her.

"Where to lady?" he asked.

Safia reluctantly gave him the address. It was 11 p.m. and visiting hours were long over. The receptionist would surely turn her away, and if she did, Safia would come right home and chalk it up to bad TV and greasy snack food, but when Safia entered the hospital there was no one at the reception desk. Safia walked right on by and pressed the elevator button.

She stood waiting for the elevator shivering in a way that had nothing to do with the temperature. She was here and she couldn't take it back. Safia took the elevator up to the seventh floor and round the corner. At any moment she would be caught. Someone would notice her and tell her to come back tomorrow, but everyone glanced over her not wondering what a girl wearing a jacket over pink hello kitty pajamas and a scrunchy in her hair was doing at this hour. What would my shrink say if he knew I was here?

Something caught Safia's eye and she ducked into a corner. It was someone she knew; camel coat, expensive haircut and prada loafers...it was Aidan. What was he doing here? She watched close behind as he entered her sister's room. Safia waited outside. He was there nearly ten minutes before he left. Safia hid behind a doorway so he wouldn't see her as he left.

She is close enough that she could reach out and touch him. She inhales. She can smell his expensive cologne. How strange it all feels. It is only when he is completely gone and nothing of him lingers that she makes her way to Laila's room.

It is amazing how beautiful she still is, who would not want to stand here and stare at her for an eternity. Something made Aidan come back here tonight. Her heart sinks and her spine tingles with fear, perhaps Aidan has fallen in love with her. She holds Laila's hand but it feels cold...distant. She can't have him, Safia thinks. God, help me she can't have him.

Laila looks like she is ready to gloat and although no words can come out of her mouth, her sister's silent laughter rings inside her ears. It is so shrill and piercing that Safia must put her hands over her ears. Even after Safia leaves, it never completely goes away.

~

CHAPTER TWENTY FIVE

Sometimes a bitter wind goes through the garden and leaves its delicate flowers blue with frost, shivering...dying. The wind with all its spite seems to have come out of nowhere. Aidan could not deny it, there was a chill in the air as poignant as any frost and it was coming from Safia's direction. It started with missed calls and unreturned messages and progressed to canceled lunches and rain checks that were never cashed.

It had been three weeks since he had seen Safia, and Aidan had enough experience with women to know when he was being frozen out. There was no point in calling her again. He had to see her in person. Displaying more confidence than he felt, he visited Corbette Advertising. He was sitting in reception restlessly flipping through a magazine when the receptionist called Safia to let her know a client was here to see her. It took nearly ten minutes for her to appear and Aidan was wondering if she would leave him sitting here.

Probably not, the little voice in the back of his mind told him. Jack Westland was way too important a client.

His patience was rewarded when Safia came down to the waiting area. She was wearing a blouse of deep aubergine over a charcoal black skirt. Her hair hung loose over her shoulders. He felt a flutter in his stomach and gave her an uneasy smile.

"Sorry, to keep you waiting. I was in the middle of a client presentation."

"No problem," said Aidan.

"What are you doing here...did we have a date?"

"Not exactly, I came to take you to lunch."

"Aidan, thanks that's really sweet but I have a ton of work. I'm..."

"Swamped...? Safia please, I don't mind waiting."

Safia felt like the biggest jerk. She owed him an apology and at the very least she owed him an explanation. Just when Safia was gathering her thoughts, and she thought things couldn't get any worse Maya LaCasse came strolling into the reception area. Oh my God, let me die now, thought Safia.

Maya, who was never one to miss an opportunity to schmooze a client, gave Aidan a juicy smile and then Safia a very quizzical look. "Aidan, what a delightful surprise. How can I help you?"

"Aidan just dropped by to approve some print ads, we sent him last week," says Safia.

"Ya, they're right here in my briefcase," says Aidan making a show of looking through his things.

"You know what? I think I left it at my office. I'll just shoot you an email."

"Aidan wait, have you had lunch?" asks Maya.

"Just grabbed a sandwich on the way over, would love to next time though."

"I'll hold you to it," said Maya stepping into the elevator and glancing at her phone having already moved on to other business.

"Thanks for covering for me," said Safia.

"About lunch?"

"A girl's gotta eat."

The restaurant was nice, the type of sit down place where people went to talk. The lighting was not too bright and the ambiance not too lively. Aidan ordered a sandwich and Safia spent an inordinate amount of interest in the menu before finally choosing the cheese tortellini in a pink sauce. Left face to face, they found there was not much to say, each testing the waters with trivial pleasantries.

Aidan felt the best way to break the ice was with a joke and when she laughed he was reminded of why he felt the way he did about her. He had been around the block enough times to know what he felt about her was different and that if he let this slip away he would regret it.

"Tell me what I did wrong?"

"What," said Safia. She felt her guard dropping. She wanted to believe that he was interested in her, and that they had something, but Laila's shadow kept lurking in the background and she felt her heart freezing up.

"Tell me what I need to apologize for and don't say it's not you, it's me. You're a better person than that."

"Look Aidan, I like you a lot, more than I imagined, but…"

"But what?"

"I can't compete with her. I just can't."

"What are you talking about?"

"Aidan, I saw you. I saw you go into Laila's hospital room one night. What were you doing there?"

It was way worse that Aidan ever imagined. He had done a lot of stupid things in his life but this was beyond stupid. How could he ever explain this without sounding like a psycho.

"Look Safia, I don't know how to explain it. I just needed to see her again. There's something about her."

"Aidan are you in love with her?"

Aidan looked like someone had punched him in the gut. His mouth opened for a second but nothing came out. He looked like a deer caught in the head lights. He was dripping with guilt. Safia did not give Aidan a chance to respond.

"Never mind. Don't answer that," said Safia getting up to leave.

"No, wait just a second. Let me explain."

"It's too late," said Safia hurrying out of the restaurant."

"Safia wait. I'm…I'm in love with you," but Safia was already out the door and Aidan was presented with the sad, quizzical look of the waiter.

Safia was in the den at Hinna's parent's house. She was sitting on the couch, legs tucked underneath her. The sofa was so plush, it looked like she would just sink right into it and that's exactly what Safia wanted to do…sink into something soft and comfortable, draw the covers over her head, and not get up.

Instead, she was doing her best on concentrating on Hinna's intricate seating chart and ticking off items on the wedding list. A bowl of plain popcorn and rice crackers lay on the coffee table. It was all Hinna would snack on until the wedding. Her fanatic low calorie diet was driving everyone crazy.

"She's not eating real food," her mother would lament. For the past few weeks, Hinna had been living off of salads, protein shakes, and other food like substances.

"At least give Safia some real food," said Rosina.

"I'm fine auntie. I like popcorn…really."

"Well, just in case you feel like something else," said Rosina putting down a plate of cookies on the coffee table.

Hinna glanced at Safia and rolled her eyes, "Seriously, I think she's trying to sabotage me."

Safia was inclined to agree as the cookies looked like they just came out of the oven, they were chocolate chip, and the chocolate was still gooey and liquid inside, and above all else, they smelled like heaven. Rice cakes or cookies…no contest, thought Safia grabbing a cookie. Comfort food. As soon as Safia bit into the warm chocolate she felt a little less miserable. If only she could bottle this feeling.

"That's the happiest, I've seen you look all day," said Hinna.

"I think I'm just tired and overworked…with your wedding and all."

"No, it's more than that, you look like a little sad...a little low on energy."

Safia practically flinched. She felt like someone had punched her in the solar plexus. She had to choke back her tears. Since when was Hinna so astute?

"Don't worry Safia your day will come. Aidan seems really great and I didn't want to say so before but I think he might even be the one."

"Thanks, but I wouldn't go far. In fact, I don't even think we're right for each other anymore."

"Why, did something happen Safia?"

Safia could feel her face turning red. She looked down and was about to mumble a response when the doorbell rang. Apparently, it was Hinna's sister, Maha, who answered it because she came in not a moment later carrying a large box.

"It's here," she said.

It could only be one thing.

"My wedding dress," exclaimed Hinna.

Hinna took the box from Maha and put it on the floor. She opened the lid. There was a lot of tissue paper but underneath was a neatly folded gown. Hinna unfolded the langha. It was beautiful, the deepest shade of red ever seen and heavily embroidered in antique gold.

"You have to try it on," said Safia.

Hinna needed no further urging. She took the wrapped items and went into the bathroom. A moment later she returned completely transformed. The dress fit perfectly and Hinna looked not only beautiful but also poised and regal. Hinna's mother had walked in the room as well, everyone just stood there staring. Rosina auntie was wiping tears from her eyes. Even Laila had never looked this beautiful, thought Safia.

"Why's everyone so quiet?" asked Hinna.

"You just look so amazing," said Safia and then added, "Tariq's mouth is going to drop."

"Good, because he's not seeing me in this dress until the big day."

"Come now, let's put this dress away before it gets dirty," said Rosina.

Safia helped Hinna take the dress off and carefully put it in her closet.

"I can't believe my big day is just around the corner. We have so much work to do."

"Don't worry Hinna, it'll get done. I have a lot more spare time now."

"Hey, what's going on with that? We have to talk about it."

"Ya we will, but right now I gotta get home before it gets too late. I'll call you tomorrow."

"Make sure you do," said Hinna unconvinced. "You know I love you," she said giving Safia a big hug.

It was with a sense of defeat that Safia came back to the stone building. It felt like Laila had won and as she approached the hospital that now appeared so solid and as impenetrable as any prison the feeling got even stronger. There he was with his horned rimmed glasses and expectant eyes ready to hear about her progress. Safia hated to admit failure especially when her last couple sessions with her shrink had proved so fruitful. He would ask what happened,

Safia honestly didn't know. How could she explain to him that it felt like she had lost, that she had been engaged in a battle of which she wasn't even aware.

In the end she didn't need to say anything. One look at her face said it all. God, she was such an open book. She had glanced at her reflection on her way over and it was nothing to smile about. Her eyes looked tired and sunken, her skin has lost its luster and her hair hung limply in a ponytail. Only a moron wouldn't sense that anything was wrong.

"Safia, how are you?" his voice filled with concern. It was very disarming and Safia just wanted to unload. She wanted to cry, she wanted to tell him she had taken a risk and it had blown up in her face. Instead, she bit her lip, gritted her teeth, and only told him part of what happened.

"I told Aidan I didn't think we should see each other anymore," said Safia unable to look him in the eye. Instead, she focused on his hands as he scribbled notes his gold band snug on his ring finger.

"I'm so sorry. Do you want to talk about it?" She felt like an idiot. It was almost painful to see the kindness in his eyes.

"I think he wanted me to be someone I wasn't."

"Who do you think he wants you to be?"

"I don't know…what I mean is, I feel l wasn't enough of for him."

"Weren't enough for him…Safia did something happen?"

Safia could tell by the look in his eyes that he sensed she was holding something back, that he knew she wasn't giving him the whole story.

"I took him with me once to visit my sister."

"How did it go?"

"It went fine. At least I thought it went fine at the time."

"And now you don't?"

"I sound insecure I know, but I don't want to be compared to her."

"Compared to her, how?"

At this Safia just laughed a laugh that was too old, and too bitter to belong to her.

"I know, huh? What kind of loser is threatened by a vegetable?"

"Safia you are a remarkable young woman. Why do you doubt yourself? Do you think he actually finds her more attractive?"

"I don't know…maybe. She's always had this magnetism."

"Safia have you asked him about this?"

Safia wondered if she should tell him about seeing Aidan at the hospital. She wondered how he would react. She bit her lips so hard that she drew blood. She could taste it in her mouth but she couldn't bring herself to say anything.

"Safia, remember what we've been working on in our last couple sessions."

"About opening up and not keeping everything bottled up inside," she said.

"No man is an island."

"I get that now…I really do. I understand now how by shutting people out I hurt my family and myself. I shut them out because of my anger and because of my guilt…but this is different."

"Is it Safia? Maybe you should give Aidan the benefit of the doubt."

"But, you don't know her...you have no idea."

This was all they had time for today. Regretfully she got up from the proverbial couch and wondered if she should have come clean. Before she left, Safia scheduled her next appointment with the receptionist, an older woman with wavy hair and kind eyes.

"Cheer-up," she said, "the day is bound to get better. When would you like to come in? Next week he's out town but everything's open after that."

"Oh, he and his wife are taking a vacation?"

"No, he's going to a conference. He doesn't take vacations, not since his wife died six years ago."

"Oh," said Safia "I could have sworn...okay, schedule me in for the week after next."

Alan Memorial Hospital

The last couple days have been busy, so busy that Sarah has not had much time to think about the sleeping girl. There are times when you know a patient will wake-up, and others when you know that they just won't. The sleeping girl has evoked both responses. It almost seems a farce to call her that for if Sarah had any doubts she is sure now. The girl is cognizant.

There is something about her that is very aware and very intelligent. She's been watching them. She reads their thoughts. At first Sarah thought she was crazy, that it was only in her head but now, from what she's seen and what she knows she has felt, it would be crazy not to believe.

It is for this very reason that Sarah tries to go into her room as little as possible, not even to look through the glass pane as tempting as it might be for she has seen staff stand and stare for way too long. It's not that she minds being seen as odd, it's something else. It's in the way the girl influences people. In the beginning it was a subtle as the waves the moon exerts over the ocean—but not anymore.

Things were getting a little haywire, the electric system, the computers going down, and people were on edge, tempers flared over some small thing or another. Sarah knew that it could only mean one thing. The sleeping girl was getting stronger.

CHAPTER TWENTY SIX

The day was wearing Safia down. There were revisions to do on every ad and a smug little note from Maya saying she wanted to see the revisions to the Jack Westland campaign before she sent them to Gavin. Maya was not easy to pin down these days and Gavin had wanted the changes pronto. Every time she got an email from Maya she found herself grinding her teeth. It got to the point that her jaw hurt at the end of the day.

Safia did not need anymore surprises, not today, that is until Orchid knocked on her office door. It was a timid knock and Safia missed it at first. When Safia opened the door her jaw dropped.

"Wow," was all Safia could say.

Orchid had changed her hair color. Now it gleamed a cobalt blue and she was wearing blue mascara to match. On anyone else it would have been a disaster, but on Orchid it worked like magic. The blue made her skin look like porcelain and her dark eyes seemed to sparkle. Orchid stepped inside Safia's office, giving herself a little spin.

"I know…isn't it awesome! My roommate is a genius."

"Oh my God, when did you decide to get it done?"

"You know my mate is a hairstylist and we were hanging out and we got a little tipsy and we got a little adventurous and before I knew it…I had a new hair color."

"Blue is your color. You should try adding a little sparkle to it, you know for Hinna's wedding."

"That would look pretty cute. Maybe, you should go blue too and then we could be twins."

"Oh my God, Hinna would so kill me."

"I know, but it would be worth it to see the expression on her face."

It was enough to make Safia smile. "That might be worth it," said Safia.

"Think about it," said Orchid plopping down on Safia's couch. "What funky color would you choose if you could choose any outrageous color you wanted?"

Safia spun her color wheel. She watched the colors spin round and round.

"I don't know, if I could go with any color…I think I would go with, red."

"Red, I like it," said Orchid.

"Not, just any red…chestnut or mahogany."

"I love it! I know how about a dark cherry."

"Ya, that would show everyone."

"I'm not kidding," said Orchid pulling out her cell. "I know a place, couple blocks away. Let's see if we can get an appointment."

"Are you serious?"

"Deadly," said Orchid pulling out her phone. "You're in luck. They have a cancellation. We'll take it. Don't worry. Sometimes a cut and a little color can change your world."

"OK, I'm in but I gotta get these revisions done before I leave, or Maya is going to kill me."

"Don't chicken out," said Orchid heading out the door.

Safia spent the rest of the afternoon in front of her computer tweaking a copy and making subtle changes to color and imagery. She was almost done. She had three versions to show Maya. She rang Maya's office for the second time but got no answer. It was just like her not to pick-up when Safia needed to head out early. Safia checked her phone. There was a message from Aidan that she didn't think she could bear listening to right now and a text from Hinna.

Safia picked up the phone to call Maya again when there was a tap at the door. Orchid let herself in. "Time's up," she said.

"I'm done. I just gotta show Maya these prints and I can't get a hold of her."

"Why don't we stop by her office. If she's not there leave them on her desk and send her a message."

"Never realized you could be so sensible Orchid."

"When it comes to getting out of here, I'm like Rainman."

"Let's go," said Safia.

Maya's office was deep within the department. It was where all the higher ups lived and usually very quiet. Today there was a lot of chatter in the area. They were probably pitching some client – getting readdy for a beauty contest. Safia knocked on Maya's door and waited, no answer. She put her ear to the door and heard some shuffling around and a moan. She knocked again.

"Just put the file on her desk and go," said Orchid.

Slowly Safia opened the door…and gasped.

"What is it?" Asked Orchid popping her head in, but Safia had lost her voice. Safia just froze, there wasn't much she could see beyond Art Fishman's bare butt bopping up and down. They were on Maya's desk. Art's pants were around his ankles and Maya's blouse was open, her well endowed breasts threatening to spill out of her bustier. Don't people lock doors, thought Safia, when she had finally regained her senses.

From the sound of their groaning they seem to have arrived at a crucial moment in their lovemaking and Safia did not want them to know them to know she was there.

"We better go," whispered Safia.

"One second," said Orchid snapping a photo with her phone, "insurance."

It was later, much later that Safia began shaking, with laughter. They were early for their appointment, having run out of Corbette as fast as they could. Safia and Orchid were sitting in a comfortable chair in a chic hair salon trying to act composed but failing miserably. A book of hair color was laid out before them, but every time they seemed to have grasped an ounce of composure, one of them would burst out laughing.

"I can't get that image out of my head," said Safia. "Every time I close my eyes I see Art Fishman's butt. Aidan is going to die when I…"

Then Safia stopped, realizing it was going to be awhile before she saw Aidan again.

"If you don't stop laughing we're never going to choose a color," said Joanie. She was Orchid's favorite stylist at the salon. She had a color palette before her and they had agreed Safia complexion would look better in the warmer tones of coppers, honeys and browns, rather than reds.

"Do you think they saw us?" asked Safia.

"Probably not, they were going at it pretty hard," said Orchid. "I just hope they never find out about my picture."

"You did not," said Joanie covering her mouth. "You are pure evil my, love."

"It's my best trait."

"If only she would use her powers for good," said Safia.

"So, what are you going to do with it? Are you going to post it?" asked Joanie.

"Don't you dare Orchid. It'll be the end of your career," said Safia.

"I think I'll keep it…for protection. Let's say, hypothetically speaking, I was caught dating a client," she winked at Safia, "and Maya got all up in my face, well now I have something to shove in her face."

Safia turned red with embarrassment.

"Orchid, you don't need to worry about me. I'm not seeing Aidan anymore."

"That's what I heard, but he's been really good for you. I don't think you should give up on this guy."

"It's complicated," said Safia.

"Sweetheart it always is," said Joanie.

"Hey, if you're hair color turns out fabulous, and I bet it will, promise me you'll reconsider about Aidan."

"With the right hair color you can do anything," said Joanie giving Safia the color palette. The colors all looked so tempting. Safia felt like a kid at a candy store. Finally, they chose highlights in a rich shade of caramel and a new, hipper haircut.

When the stylist was done, the effect was breathtaking. Safia barely recognized herself.

"We've got to show you off over drinks," said Orchid.

It was around that time where anyone that didn't want to go home would be huddled around a table in the old watering hole, as Orchid liked to call it.

"Now don't come in until I text you," she said leaving Safia outside the door.

When Orchid gave the word, Safia came from around the corner with a sweeping, "ta-da."

It was suddenly very quiet. Perhaps they were trying to recognize me, thought Safia. Neal was the first to speak.

"OMG, we got a diva in the house."

It was true. Safia couldn't stop looking at her reflection, a whole new person stared back. The cut was very bold, almost but not quite to the point of being edgy. Her hair was still medium length but now she had layers around her face and the edges were tapered and razor cut, with long side sweeping bangs and all that rich color—two different shades of caramel swept through her hair blending seamlessly and giving the illusion of depth and a richness she hadn't possessed before.

"First round is on me guys," said Safia.

Today she would not hurry home. Today she would stay and see where the night led. Today she would dance until dawn.

"That's my party girl," said Orchid and then added. "Wait until Hinna gets a load of you."

Aidan thought he was done with places like this. He thought he was done with feeling sorry for himself. Guess somethings never change. He was sitting at bar and nursing a drink he didn't really want with no plans for the night. The after work crowd has just started coming in. People in twos and threes clustered over tables drinking fancy beers, when someone caught his eye.

Not the companion he would have hoped for, but beggars couldn't be choosers. He took a closer look. Yup, he'd know that movie star smile anywhere, perfectly coiffed hair, not a beautiful blonde lock out of place. What harm would it do to share a drink with someone that was making him rich by the minute.

"Mind if I join you?" asked Aidan.

Jack Westland smiled good naturedly. He was wearing khakis and a rust colored shirt and in his hand he had a beverage that looked red and fruity.

"Unless, you're expecting someone else?" asked Aidan.

"No not at all, please do pull up a seat. I'm waiting for a writer that wanted to talk about the book, but he's running late," said Jack.

"I'm surprised you aren't being swarmed by all your fans."

Jack chuckled. "I think it's too dark in here for people to recognize me."

"This whole campaign has been spreading like wildfire," said Aidan.

"I want to thank you and Art for all the work you've done on my book and for setting up all the events. You don't know how many people you've touched…how many thank you letters I get and keep getting. "

"All in a days work," said Aidan.

Jack gave him an amused smile. "Is that all it is?"

"I don't know…seemed like a good business opportunity. Fish sometimes bets on the wrong horse, but this time, I gotta admit he nailed it."

"Let me ask you something, why do you endorse something you are not sure you believe in?" And then after a pause. "I've seen you at the events and I don't think you're doing this just for the money. I think you're looking for something besides money…and maybe I'm here to help you find it."

Aidan was about to scoff and tell Jack he was crazy, but instead let out a deep breath. "What if I found it, but it slipped through my fingers. What do I do then?"

"If it slipped through your fingers, think about whether it's something you really want? And if it is, regroup and try again. Follow the signs."

"You know, you're not as crazy as I thought you were," said Aidan putting cash down on the table. Maybe he would do something different tonight instead of drowning his problems.

Fittingly, it had started to rain. Fat little rain drops splashed on his windshield. It matched his dismal mood. Up ahead he saw the warm glow of lights and decided to stop. The warmth of the store drew him in. Music played softly in the background. A multitude of Jack's books lined the display window. A couple people had picked-up Jack's book. Good. It was one of those big chains that had driven out all the independent book stores, that were slowing going under themselves. Yet, from the crowd of people inside you would never know it. Is this what everyone else did on a Friday night?

Aidan smiled, Jack had said to look for a sign and this was as good as any. Aidan listened closely, it was jazz — the peppy voice of Sinatra. It made him think of Safia. He could picture her listening to his music, late at night...hunched over her computer and old blue eyes playing in the background.

Aidan started, perusing first through the self-help—a good a place to start as any—and then finance and investing. After he had picked apart these sections he found it more interesting to people watch. Many were young, smartly dressed, probably over-educated and most definitely underpaid. He could picture Safia here, with her friends walking in the door at any moment. It wasn't too far from her work.

Not wanting to leave yet, Aidan got in line for coffee. It was a long line and moving slowly and he was left with an inordinate amount of time to look at the menu. The ding on his phone was almost a relief. He retrieved from his pocket and that's when he saw it, old blue eyes, staring back at him. Had he not heard the ding of his phone, he might've missed it. He grabbed the CD and paid for it and his coffee.

The message was from Fish, asking if he was up for dinner. It was a place at the other end of town. Why not? thought Aidan walking back to the car. He put the CD in his glove compartment and sent Fish a text back: *Sounds good, be there in half an hour.*

CHAPTER TWENTY SEVEN

Safia stumbled out of a packed taxi nearly hitting her head on the sidewalk. She said goodbye to her friends and wobbled to the front door. She wondered if she was going to be able to make it to her apartment. Inside the elevator, she felt a little woozy and after she got off, the long hallway felt endless. Once inside her small flat she was able to make it to her bed, where she dropped like a ton of bricks and there she rest sounder than the dead—*sounder than even me.*

Safia slept through her alarm, still not believing the ray of light that filtered through her curtains. It just made her want to grab her blanket and shove it over her head and cocoon herself until she was ready to get up, which would not be for a while. Eventually, it was not the sunshine but the voices that broke through her slumber. The voices that would not be quiet. She did not understand why they were talking, and what in hell they had to be so cheerful about until she raised her head and listened carefully to the radio. Her alarm had gone off and she hadn't realized it. She looked at the time. It was 11 a.m. She had overslept by an hour. What was that queasy feeling that she felt in her stomach…oh yes, panic.

Safia untangled herself from her sheets. She was still in last night's clothes. She caught a glimpse of herself in the mirror and jumped back. Her edgy new hair stood in spikes and tangles and the color looked garish in the sunlight — Halloween punk. If she was going for vampire in a rock band, she had the right look. No time to dwell on her scary image. She needed to jump into the shower, grab coffee, pull a cap over her head, and go. Hinna was going to be so pissed if Safia made her late for her own wedding.

When she arrived at Hinna's parent's house, it was controlled chaos. There were half a dozen out of towners, that were staying with them and would be attending the wedding. The same group of kids were again running all over the place. Hinna's mom answered the door, still dressed in her bathrobe.

"Thank God, you're here. Everyone is running late and Hinna is freaking out."

Safia climbed up the stairs and knocked on Hinna's room before entering. A beautician was there to help get Hinna ready. She had already helped Henna into the gown. Her hair and make-up still needed to be done. She hadn't put on any jewelry and last of all, the heavy dupetta (stole) laden with embroidery needed to be fitted and pinned onto her.

"Where were you?" asked Hinna frantically, and then "What happened to your hair?" as Safia pulled the cap off.

"I got a haircut…and some color," explained Safia, her face was turning red. She knew she looked horrid.

"You got something," said Hinna. "Hurry-up and change into your outfit. You can have your hair done while they are working on my make-up."

Safia went into the bathroom and changed into her langha. Just putting on the silky green gown made her feel better. The material was soft, heavy, and draped smoothly around her body. The color made her look a little fresher, not so tired and worn out. When she came out there was a stylist waiting to do her hair. She sat in the chair and the stylist started running her finger through Safia's hair. At first it felt really good and then she started snagging on all the tangles. After her hair was combed and smoothed out, she ran a curling iron through it.

Safia had delicate features so they decided on an up-do that was soft and romantic with lots of loose tendrils falling out and shaping her face. The effect was gorgeous.

"Wow," said Maha. "You're going to be beating them off with a stick."

"She totally is," said Hinna. "I love that color on you."

"Thanks," said Safia looking at herself in the mirror, lost in her own reflection.

"Okay, I'm next," said Maha sitting down to get her hair done. She was wearing a beautiful langha (gown) in a dusty rose. She already had her makeup done. This time it was very natural and demure, a look that suited her better than the garish paint she usually wore. While Safia was getting her make-up done, she watched as the stylist did Maha's hair. She needed to concentrate on something to prevent her from yawning. The stylist expertly put Maha's hair half-up with a wavy side ponytail. It looked perfect. Maha was well on her way to being a heartbreaker.

Rosina auntie popped her head in, and was pleased that they were almost ready. Looking at her watch, she noted, "The groom's family is supposed to arrive any minute for the vows, which is going to be a small family event." Sofia could tell that she was scared to death that they would be on time. But, they actually arrived an hour late.

When Tariq's family shows up the imams (priests) have already been waiting for fifteen minutes. The two imams are both dressed identically in long cloaks, skull caps, and beards, the main difference being the imam representing Hinna is an elderly gentlemen, his beard a fluffy grey. The younger imam is representing Tariq in the marriage contract.

The bride and groom are in different parts of the house during the vows. Hinna waits in her room with Safia, Maha, her mother, and her aunt. The imam will come to her for her vows, while Tariq waits with the male members of his family. Hinna's bedroom has been partitioned with a delicate makeshift curtain to separate the imam from the women. When it is Hinna's turn, the imam comes upstairs. He is on one side of the curtain while the women remain on the other side. As tradition dictates, he asks Hinna three times if she consents to the marriage contract—giving her three chances to back out. The groom is asked only once. The vows are done quickly and solemnly.

Safia gives Hinna and her aunt a big hug. There are tears in Rosina's eyes. For the next fifteen minutes there is much hugging and congratulating, until Maha looks at her watch.

"We need to hurry or we'll be late for the photo shoot."

The wedding party departs for a second location. Hinna has picked out the ideal place. A historic mansion with winding staircases, marble floors and lush gardens — *I wait for them.*

CHAPTER TWENTY EIGHT

I do not intend to be excluded...not today.

I wander through this palace and take in the smell of freshly polished wood, the gleam of marble. Oh, how the chandelier must sparkle at night. I glide over the rich carpets, the antique furniture, the exquisite art, and make my mark in every room. I could get used to a place like this. I have learned every corner, every crevice of this palace, but it is not likely that I may become its mistress.

I will not trade one prison for another, even one as beautiful as this. It is because I know they will arrive soon. Today, I intend to stand amongst them, to walk side by side, and at every turn they will feel my presence. They will hear me whisper...he is mine, give him to me.

They will never feel warm, even as the bright rays of the sun shine down upon them. They will feel me alongside them and shiver. When the wind blows, they will hear my laughter. When they taste their food, it is my bitterness that will seep through. When they drink, their thirst will not be quenched...not until I find relief. They cannot hide from me, not in their fine clothes and expensive cars.

I look out the window. I can see far into the distance. I want to smile. This day belongs to me, and I am excited.

The estate was painted in pale greys and whites, and appeared to gleam against the sunlight, the lawn, a blanket of green. Safia got out of the car and stood for a moment scarcely believing it was real. It made her feel small if as if they were not grand enough to disturb such a place, as if they were intruders and not guests.

Still, she is the first to get out of the car and once she does, she becomes very still. She listens to something in the air and then gazes up to the balcony, heavy drapes conceal a window. The window is at a choice location, one that would allow it to survey the grounds and take them all in. The sound of voices breaks her concentration. Hinna and Tariq step out of a limo.

Tariq is wearing a royal blue sherwani accented with gold, every bit the prince beside Hinna. They look like a couple that has jumped out of India's history pages. Hinna's wedding langha is very vintage, an old world style that she wears well. Her jewelry is brilliant with a gold choker that spans the width of her chest and it is accented with shimmering rubies. Her hair, in its elaborate up-do, is elegant. Her dupatta is red with a thick gold border and placed three quarters of the way up her head.

Tariq holds her hand and guides her inside the mansion. The photographer is setting up his equipment and eyeing a beautiful fountain, not far on the property there is said to be a gazebo. Stepping inside you feel like you've entered another world, fallen through the fabric of time. It is not just the marble staircase, or ornate drawing rooms, and romantic terraces but the way it sits expectant...waiting for a party that is about to start.

Group pictures are set-up first so that the bridal party may leave for the reception hall, leaving Hinna and Tariq behind for some of the more romantic shots. The photographer knows what he wants from the group and they begin quickly. Gently he adjusts their clothes and directs them in what seems like a million different permutations.

Safia's smile begins to hurt and she looks forward to when this is all over so that she can start slouching again. The next series of shots is all about the groom's family and so Safia takes a moment to steal away.

She can hear Maha laughing, her voice echoes through the lobby. Safia walks into a room that looks like a parlor or a salon. There is a piano in the corner. Around the corner is a library shelved with leather bound books, a mahogany desk, and a billiards table. Further back is a staircase. Intrigued, Safia makes her way up the staircase. She knows that some of the rooms have balconies and she thinks it would be nice to have an aerial view of the estate. She wants to find the room that overlooks the entrance.

The staircase appears to wind as she steps further along. Safia doesn't like heights but there is a sense déjà vu, as if she has seen this house before, and now she is so far up that she is afraid to look down, but she does. Over the rail she sees the corridor and the rooms she has passed through. She stands as if in a trance and looks down the staircase. She has forgotten about the wedding party. There is a fragrance that reminds her of someone she cares not to think about. She feels that if she just turns around someone will be standing there facing her.

She can sense them.

She can feel spidery little fingers at the back of her neck. She grips the railing a little tighter. She hears someone call her name. She needs to get back down, but the moment she takes her first step, she feels her high heel slip and miss its mark. She is stumbling and if she's not careful this will turn into a horrendous fall. The only thing she can do is to grab the railing and hope it doesn't break. In trying to steady herself, her shoe falls off her foot. She watches it tumble to the bottom hitting every step on the way down, but she is safe, and she is steady. She sits on the steps to compose herself and takes the other high heel off. No more risks. When she comes down, Maha is at the bottom of the staircase holding the fallen shoe.

"Are you alright? You look pretty shaken up."

Safia nods.

"We're done here. Hinna and Tariq will join us later. You're riding with us to the reception," then after a pause, "what happened up there? You look a little dizzy."

Safia manages a smile, "Must be all that partying coming back to haunt me."

When Safia is safely inside the car, she can't help looking back at the house as they drive away. Hinna and Tariq are still there…alone, but it is not them she is worried about. She can see the condensation in her window that shouldn't be there at this time of year. Her aunt pulls the shawl around her a little tighter. Maha twitches and looks at her a little nervously. They are all holding their breath, but are not sure why, and then there is the blare of a horn as her uncle accidentally cuts someone off. Gradually, their unease dissipates and the journey returns to normal with her aunt re-applying lipstick and Maha fidgeting with her jewelry…and this worries her most of all.

Aidan stares at his reflection in his bedroom mirror. He can't help smiling at himself. He is dressed in a Ralph Lauren suite in a steel blue. It sets off his pale grey eyes. This time I'm ready, he thinks and then looks over his shoulder. The room looks exactly the same as it did in the mirror in front of him. Nothing is amiss and yet the sensation is there. The sensation of being watched, an eerie tingle on the back of this neck. Is there something he's missing?

I'm going nuts, he thinks. Just nerves he tells himself because he knows that she's going to be there. He's really fucked it up with Safia, but this is his chance to make things right. She hasn't responded to any of his messages, but he knows that she will be there tonight. His timing has been too bad to casually run into her after work and he's never been much of a stalker. At one point he thought he had glimpsed her and then when she turned her head, it looked like a completely different girl.

Now for the first time he knows exactly where she's going to be. There's no way she's going to miss it. She's part of the bridal party.

CHAPTER TWENTY NINE

I was made for parties.

Is there anything more romantic? The air is perfumed, the lights twinkle and the music, it floats through the room like an invisible fog. We drink it in and we are better for it. It is here that I shine best. It is here that I am in my element with beautiful people and ornate costumes, each more striking than the next.

He will be drawn here. He will see a shimmer in the air and be intrigued. He will see me — the glint in a pretty girl's eye and know that I watch him. For tonight I am no one and everyone. He will see me in the sparkle in his drink and the gleam of a precious stone, worn around a hundred necks.

I can picture the exact moment I lay eyes on him, holding his gaze with eyes that are not mine, cutting through a sea of sleeping people, drunk within their own merriment and paralyzed within their respective dreams...up and down the music churns, round and round they all go.

Tonight I will be everywhere and nowhere. No other will take him from me.

Only I am real.

Safia is the first to enter the banquet hall. She is overcome by the beauty and silence of the room. It is the sizzling, electric silence that occurs just before something erupts. What an occasion it will be. The room is gorgeous in a color scheme of red gold a white. The richness and the depth of the colors add to the Hall's mystique, as if one has stepped back in time. The stage up front is draped with curtains, and an ornate looking sofa meant for the bride and groom sits in the middle, awaiting the royal couple that will preside over the banquet. Safia wishes the stillness of the room could last forever. The sound of talking in the lobby brings Safia back to the task at hand. Work must be done.

If South Asian weddings are known for anything, it's the food. Appetizers must be prepared and ready to go. The musicians have arrived, a tabla and a sitar player are setting up in a corner of the lobby. The appetizer should be nearby so that food and music are hand in hand. Seating chart, Safia thinks. A table to greet guests and show them where they are to be seated must be set-up. Once all this is done Safia can relax.

A mere fifteen minutes later, the first guests have arrived. Soon the smell of spiced appetizers wafts through the lobby. Wedding guests dressed in rich colors mingle while munching on, chicken tikka, shish kababs, fried pakoras, and spicy fish with classical Indian music adding flavor to the background, while inside the finishing touches are being put on the dining tables.

As doors open and the guests stream in, members of the bridal party greet them. Safia catches their reactions upon entering the banquet hall. Everyone is suitably impressed. She sees Neal and Orchid enter and she gives them a little wave. At first they look at her blankly and then grin as recognition dawns. Safia gives them big hugs. Orchid who is slim and petite fits completely into Safia's arms, like a child. While even in his formal wear, Neal's rock hard muscles strain against her.

"You look like a princess," says Orchid. She is wearing a pale yellow salwar khameez (pant suit) with gold trim that Safia helped pick out. It looks adorable on her. Neal who would stand out wearing a sac looked like a demi-God dressed in a cool black corduroy dinner jacket over a steel grey turtle neck.

"You think I look good, wait until you see Hinna." "Bet she pulls off Goddess pretty well," said Neal. "You would know," says Safia. "You look like Apollo come to life."

"I prefer Aries," says Neal.

"Thought your motto was, make love not war," says Orchid.

"Sometimes love is war," says Neal.

Safia is about to add, "he need only meet his Venus," but loses her train of thought, something in the crowd catches her attention. She looks up and there he is, soft grey eyes and a generous smile and for one split second time has stood still. The room is empty. It is just the two of them, and just as easily as it came, the moment is over.

Time has moved on and Aidan has disappeared into the crowd. Safia is left confused, still searching the room, but he is no where in sight.

"Looking for someone?" Asks Neal.

"I thought I saw someone I know."

"It's going to be a long night, bet you'll find him again."

"We better get to our table," says Orchid tugging Neal's arm. "Don't worry," she adds. "I think he's looking for you too."

This is one wedding that Aidan is on time for. This may be his one chance to set things right. He knows that she will be here, she has to be. The banquet hall is large and lavish. He feels like he is on a movie set. Rich curtains of red and gold draped the pillars, subtle lighting illuminate the stage that contained a Mughal inspired love seat. The tablecloths are a deep olive green with white underneath, just the shade and the brocade on them make Aidan think they may have been custom made. The guests are dressed accordingly with women in dazzling jewelry on traditional langhas and salwar khameez. The men all looked sharp in their suits. Geez, when did weddings become so over-the-top, he thinks.

Aidan is dressed to kill tonight, and people notice. Two young women pass by. They look at him from the corner of their eyes. He can hear them giggle softly. It isn't overt, but he still feels self-conscious. He makes his way over to his table without incident. His parents are already there and he wants to ask his mom how he looks. His mother smiles at him and as if reading his mind says, "Jannu, you look so handsome. Is that a new suit?"

"This old thing," says Aidan pulling out a cocky smile that belonged to his younger days. He looks around the table. Amina and Kevan have not arrived. He sits down just in time to see his father glance at his watch. He is wearing the silver Rolex, Amina got him for his birthday. It glitters and seems to catch the light. Amina has never been subtle, but his father seems to like it well enough—better than the golf lessons Aidan got him. They seem impressed that he's arrived on time. His mother gives him a sly smile, but his father as usual is clueless.

"Looking for someone?" she asks.

"Just hoping to run into a friend," he says

His father is looking at him quizzically. "Don't leave before they serve dinner," he adds.

"Wouldn't dream of it," says Aidan letting out a long drawn out breath. The place is huge and she is nowhere to be seen. His parents are munching contently and schmoozing with every third person that walks by. The smell of food reminds him that he's hungry, might as well enjoy the party, he thinks deciding to grab some appetizers. He has tread no more than four or five steps when someone calls out his name.

Harris Ali is giving him a big smile and shaking his hand. Aidan remembers him from college. He used to play tennis. He's become a little thicker since his twenties and his hair is thinning. Harris gives him a slap on the back and handshake that is a little too firm and a little too enthusiastic, as if he's trying to prove something. According to his business card he's in consulting. On his way to the buffet table Aidan runs into half a dozen more acquaintances and several young women have given him shy and not so shy smiles. In fact, one young woman is smiling quite brazenly at him. It unnerves him a little until he realizes where he knows her from. He knew her in high school; he hung out with her brother. She sees the recognition in his eyes.

"How are you?" she asks.

"Wow, look at you all grown up," and is she ever. Gone is the chubby little girl, with frizzy hair, that was all cheeks and dimples. In its place is a killer body, with long sleek hair but the adorable dimples remain. "Time moves on," she says flipping her hair.

Wow, she's actually flirting with him.

"You're telling me. I can't get over you."

"You don't look so bad yourself," she says, "are you living in the city?" but before he has a chance to answer fully she hands him a business card.

"Stay in touch," she says.

Aidan takes the card, a little embarrassed. Six months ago, he would've patted himself on the back and felt like he was back in the game. Now he realizes that games are for children and he's not a kid anymore. No more diversions. He scans the crowd. The lighting is dim and all the faces blend into one another. He's come this far and still she eludes him, but not for long. Something catches his eye, something blue. Bull's-eye.

The two people sitting at the next table are unmistakable. The sparkly blue hair acts like a beacon in a sea of brunettes. As recognition sets in, he makes a beeline for Safia's co-workers. They haven't been formally introduced, but he knows them and he suspects that they know about him as well. As he approaches, he sees them whispering to each other. He has caught them in the middle of a private conversation or a private joke, judging from the chuckles.

"How's it going?" he says

They look up surprised and Aidan wonders if they recognize him. Orchid gives him a mischievous smile but it's Neal that responds.

"Great man, just taking in the party."

"Yeah, it's something, isn't it?"

"Love the food," says Orchid. "I think I'm gonna have Indian food at my wedding."

"I don't mean to interrupt," say Aidan hesitantly, "but have you seen Safia?"

"You mean you haven't seen her?" asks Orchid. Aidan wonders if he's missing something.

"There she is," says Neal. "She's walking towards the exit."

"She changed her hair. She's wearing the green outfit and shoulder length hair with toffee highlights. I'm so jealous," adds Orchid.

"Not everyone can pull off sapphire," says Neal. "Hmmm...true," ponders Orchid, but before she can continue Aidan has made his exit.

"Thanks, I'll see if I can catch-up with her," says Aidan as he dashes across the room. He wants to reach her before anyone else, but as he approaches, he wonders if he's been trailing the right girl. There are so many women wearing green, and there is much about her that appears different from afar. Not just the way she looks, but the way she moves.

Suddenly she stops, or at least someone has stopped her and she is absorbed in conversation. Aidan hasn't gotten a good look at her yet. He is only a few feet away and he is still not sure if it's really her. Something about her is different. He circles around so that he can see her face. It's the same girl, but it isn't.

Everything about her seems different…in this setting, in this light. People keep passing by, obstructing his view. He wants to call out to her but she's so absorbed with the person before her that he's not sure she'd hear him. He feels invisible. He is so close to her that he could reach out and touch her hand, but he doesn't. Her friend has left and for an instant she is alone. He wants to call her name but he is drowned out by the sound of the microphone.

Safia has just spent ten minutes listening to an out of town relative complain about the seating plan. She thinks they can add a place setting to one of the other tables or perhaps someone might be willing to switch. She is still contemplating the best solution when she hears someone call her name, but she doesn't know where to look. So many people all seem to need her at the same time. She hears the sound of the mic and realizes it's time to go back to her seat. Before she returns, she looks around one more time for the voice she thought she heard. There is no one there, just the lingering scent of cologne, as if someone has just left.

Tariq's best man is center stage. He taps the microphone and Aidan can hear it crackle. It makes him flinch.

"Ladies and Gentleman, please take your seat so that we may welcome the bride and groom."

Guests hastily go back to their tables. Aidan looks back at where he left Safia, but she is gone. As Aidan head's back to his family's table, he sees that Amina and Kevan have arrived. Amina is dressed in a rich burgundy, pale face, prominent lipstick. He looks at Kevan and smiles at his tie. She's picked out a tie that matches her outfit, leave it to Amina.

He's about to say hello, when the silence is broken by a Bollywood love song coming through the speakers. The bride and groom enter, tall and proud, and breathtakingly beautiful, their exquisiteness draws people in and holds their gaze as they walk to the front of the room. All eyes are upon them...all eyes except Aidan's.

CHAPTER THIRTY

Am I so evil?

I see him, and I know that he doesn't belong to me—but he probably should. She may look like me, but she is not as beautiful. She may move like me, but she is not as graceful. I can always be someone else... although it's much more fun to be me.

It is not as though I have never felt regret. I feel regret every day. I regret the spinning of that damned wheel. I take a deep breath. I can feel the beating of his heart as if it were inside my own skin. I have a chance now to right my wrongs to gain back all that I have lost...or so the old woman keeps telling me.

My one consolation is that he is here now. He is so close. I feel him climbing through the thickets of my castle surrounded by an unimaginable jungle—preda-tors lurking in the distance. It is his destiny that waits for him within these decrepit walls.

There are many distractions. He has not yet reached the entrance to the gate, but he will. He can't help but be drawn to me. He doesn't know what pulls him or what awaits—but I do. It is a prophecy that has been foretold, the old woman has promised me this—and she will lead him right to it

Destiny is overrated. For a long time now Safia had a loose premonition about this day, this day that should belong to her cousin Hinna and it does. It was a beautiful reception, absolutely royal, but in a way it was also the day Safia had chosen to come out—like a butterfly. She had wrapped herself up in a cocoon for so many years and now she had finally emerged with new hair and new clothes all glammed up to take her place in society.

Family members had smiled approvingly, more distant relatives had been suitably impressed. The day was one that should have been cataloged and filed under success, if only it wasn't for that ache. That ache inside her that felt like defeat. She hadn't spoken to Aidan all evening and when their eyes finally met, he seemed to look away, as if she were a stranger. I've really done it this time, she thinks.

Safia felt tired and she looked even worse. Her feet hurt, her outfit was a little disheveled, her hair falling out and her makeup worn out and smudged, Cinderella after the ball. Any minute now her car would turn into a pumpkin. She was about to check her watch... see how close she was to midnight, when she felt a tap on her shoulder. It was her aunt. Her aunt still had her party face on. She had been doing this a lot longer than Safia.

"Be a dear and go see how your grandmother is doing," she said. Her voice was a little strained. "She's probably been left alone for hours."

Safia looked around. She could see her grandmother a couple tables away. She is wearing a dusty blue sari that sparkles underneath the chandeliers. Everyone that was seated with her has wandered off. Her tea is finished and her cake is untouched. Safia felt a pang of guilt. It is easy to forget about her in the hustle and bustle of the night. Her grandmother, patient woman that she is, never seems to mind.

Safia walks over and gives her grandmother a hug.

"Can I get you anything?" She asks.

Her grandmother kisses her on the cheek. "No, I've had my fill today, love. Go ask your cousin Samir to take me home. I am tired and I feel very old tonight."

"Let me wrap that slice of cake for you. You can have it in the morning," said Safia.

"Always such a sweet girl."

Safia picks up the cake and sends her cousin a text. Moments later, they are in the lobby waiting for his car to pull up. Samir is tall and thick with a goofy smile but always good natured. He comes around to help his grandmother into the car. He opens the back door and Safia helps her into the seat making sure that the pleats of her sari are tucked inside. After the door has been closed and she is safely inside he says, "I'll get you home in a flash."

He can see her eyes in his rearview mirror. They do not look tired, in fact they burn with much intensity.

"No, there is somewhere else I want to go first," she says.

For the first time he feels a sense of unease, but then she tells him the location and as strange as it is, he thinks he understands.

Alan Memorial Hospital

Sarah takes a deep breath and listens. She listens to the silence and tries to gauge what type of night it will be. All signs points to a slow night, but there is something in the air. The hair on Sarah's neck stands onend. At the back of mind she hears a buzz...electricity. She knows that buzz well from her nights working as an ER nurse. It's been a long time but her instincts are still there. It's the type of buzz that foreshadows a horrific accident, and she's tempted to warn the ER.

The phone rings and she nearly jumps. They have the wrong department but nearly bite her head off as she transfers the call. Everyone's on edge today. This is the third time tonight someone has growled at her. She takes a deep breath and ignores it. Still, she can feel it lurking. It's hiding in the night. It's hiding in the silence.

Her mind wanders to the sleeping girl. She has the nagging feeling that she should check on her. It's a feeling she has learned to trust. She makes a mental note to pop in when she is doing her rounds. She needs to finish some paperwork first.

When she finally looks into her room, she appears to be sleeping peacefully. Sarah steps a little closer. A shadow has fallen on her face. She feels it too, thinks Sarah. She's still trying to read the girl's face when something breaks her concentration. It's a whisper. Almost as if someone's standing directly behind her, but when she turns around no one's there.

The sleeping girl offers no explanation and Sarah hurries back to her station and begins to absorb herself in her work. Still, the warning lingers in the back her mind—someone's coming.

It is the point in the evening when the lights have dimmed, the cake has been cut, dinner is long over and guests are lingering over their dessert, a four-tier, lemon cake with buttercream icing, and taking their last sip of coffee. Safia licks her lips with satisfaction. The huge piece of cake was divine with just the right amount of sweet and tartness. The faint fragrance of lemon still clings to Safia's fork and she lets out a long, wistful sigh. She's thinking of him and looking around the room.

She wants to catch his eye one more time in spite of how her look has fallen apart, but something has kept her firmly in her seat. It's not just that she has noticed him, she's noticed him mingling...making the rounds. She's noticed the surety of his gait and the breadth of his smile, that seems to draw people to him, too many people—too many women—looking up at him, batting their eyelashes and twirling their hair, letting him know how welcome they are to meet him. Has she lost him forever?

And then something changes. Inadvertently, Safia starts tapping her foot. The music now has a little more oomph. The beat is contagious and people start getting into the rhythm, tapping their feet and imagining the possibilities of the night. The DJ calls everyone's attention to the dance floor. The bride and groom will begin the evening with the first dance. The music is fast-paced and for someone wearing ten pounds of jewelry, Hinna is doing pretty well. Tariq is following along somewhat awkwardly. Everyone else is bouncing around in their seat, like they have an itch they can't seem to scratch. It doesn't take long for the other guests to join Hinna and Tariq. The energy in the room has shot up by two hundred percent.

Safia sees bright blue hair bopping around. Orchid is flying around like a fairy. Her partner is a little guy in his early teens who's having the time of his life with her. Hinna's sister, Maha, is dancing with a group of girls and even Neal has risked his ultra cool image and is shimmying to the music. Safia is watching from the edge of the dance floor not knowing whether to dive in, or sit it out. Neal gives her a wink that makes her feel like she should get in there.

The song ends and the next song is a little slower. Neal goes back to his seat. She notices with a pang that ripples through her that he's sitting next to Aidan. They are speaking to each other, but Safia is too far away to hear what they are saying.

"Are you going to stare at her all evening," says Neal taking a sip of his drink.

"You're not asking the right questions my friend," says Aidan giving him a cynical smile that makes Neal wonder if he is mocking him or himself.

"What's the right question then?"

"The right question is," says Aidan, "do I have a plan?"

"Sometimes spontaneity exudes the best plan," says Neal. Aidan looks slightly defeated.

"I've gone over it in my head a million different ways and can't think of anything I haven't said."

"So, don't say anything, Bro...just dance."

Aidan wants to laugh. He remembers what's been bothering him about Safia all evening and that it's not that she doesn't look like herself. It's that she looks so much like someone else. Almost like watching a ghost float around the room. He doesn't need a ghost, what he needs is flesh and blood. He listens half heartedly to the music...trendy, shallow, and a little obnoxious, not exactly what he felt like dancing to, still better to act than do nothing.

"You're right," says Aidan addressing Neal. He rises from his chair and it looks like he's finally going to take the plunge...ask the dreaded question.

"But there's something I need to do first," he continues, and with that he walks away from the dance floor across the hall and out the door, not looking back. He doesn't see Neal's mouth drop, or the puzzled look on Orchid's face, or the way Safia's face has crumpled without ever shedding a tear. There is something calling him that he can't ignore.

The night air feels like freedom. Aidan fishes for his keys and tries to remember where he parked his car. He catches sight of other guests that have decided to call it a night, they carry drowsy children in their arms. His own parents left a long time ago claiming tiredness. His car is waiting for him, sleek and black. He takes one last look back at the hotel. He can still feel the party going on inside. It will go on for many hours yet.

Don't lose your nerve, he tells himself slipping into the driver's seat. He puts his keys in the ignition ready to drive off but then he looks into the glove compartment. Bulls-eye. It's right where he left it. He grins from ear-to-ear. This is going to be a night she won't forget.

Alan Memorial Hospital

Sarah had been looking over her shoulder all evening, certain she heard footsteps when no one was to be seen. It was late at night when he finally came, yet nobody questioned his appearance. He walked with a surety of someone who belonged even without his white coat. Sarah merely raised an eyebrow as he passed by her at the nurses' station.

She had seen him here many times before standing outside her door, looking longingly at the girl. Usually he came in between patients, dressed smartly in a blazer and tie, today his evening off, he was dressed casually wearing a long sleeved T-shirt and jeans. It made him look ten years younger, like the boy he had once been before life had left its mark.

He might have been difficult to recognize but as soon as Sarah saw his face and those wire-rimmed glasses, that did nothing to hide the beauty of his eyes, she waved him through. She couldn't imagine why he was here at this time of night, but she knew where he was going, even though the girl was not his patient.

"Good evening Doctor," she said matter-a-factly, covering up her nervousness. Funny thought, it's not the girl she fears for.

"Yes, it is," he says smiling back at her, as if he had every right to be there.

Sarah's eyes never leave him as he walks down the hall and into the sleeping girl's room. For the briefest second she has the urge to follow, but thinks better of it.

"Don't go," she wants to say to him. She knows too well the temptation of the sleeping girl. She has a way of claiming those that open up to her.

CHAPTER THIRTY ONE

Safia is licking her wounds. It isn't the first time she's lost a man, just the first time it's been her own doing. She's glad that the evening is at a close. The wait staff have started clearing away the dessert table and the bar is closed. Soon the bride and groom will drive off in their black stretch limo and Safia and everyone else in the bridal party will be faced with a tearful goodbye.

Orchid sits beside her, her forehead lined with perspiration with her blue hair that has fallen so far from disheveled that it has taken on a life of its own. She places her hand sympathetically on top of Safia's, who reacts merely with a shrug...you win some...you lose some.

There are items Safia should start packing into the car — boxed gifts, left over bombonieres. Perhaps she can recruit one of the boys to help with the heavy lifting. Safia is about to search out Maha and ask her to bring the car around when the music abruptly stops.

"Ladies and gentleman may I have your attention."

Safia looks up and it's Aidan holding the mic and he's looking in her direction. In fact, he's looking right at her. The room has become silent.

"Now we all know that the first dance of the evening belongs to the bride and groom, but I'm not ready to end the night without asking someone to honor me with the last dance," he says while walking towards Safia. It grew quiet before the music started again, but it was very different then the music that had previously played.

The sound of an orchestra filled the room as the dance floor cleared. The voice of Sinatra hung in the air. *Strangers in the night exchanging glances, wondering in the night; what were the chances?*

Aidan holds his hand out to her, as everyone watches silently. This isn't real she thinks, but the look in his eyes tells her it is. Safia glides into his arms amidst some appreciative claps. Soon other guests join in for one last dance, but Safia doesn't see them; they feel alone in the room.

Everything about this moment feels right — the smell of his aftershave, Aidan's arms around her, the passion in his eyes. There is only one thing she wants more…

"When I saw you leave, I thought you were gone forever. I'm glad you came back."

"So am I," says Aidan, and as he bends down, their lips meet, their bodies melt into each other, and just for a moment… time really does stand still.

CHAPTER THIRTY TWO

I felt it...that kiss.

A kiss that should have been mine. I knew the moment he touched her lips. I felt their hearts beat, thudding loudly in my ear. A thread of desire passed through my body from the top of my head, down to my fingers and toes. I am almost awake, but not quite. It is my punishment. What is it that the old woman has been whispering? A kiss will bring me back to life...slowly back to life, a life alone and unloved.

I hear footsteps. She is coming to gloat, though it is not her usual shuffle. These steps are different. They tread softly, purposely and with every step they get louder. I hear them from far away and my pulse quickens. I breathe and the musky scent of incense fills me. For a moment, I am no longer in this dreary room. I no longer feel the stiff mattress of my prison, but the plush bed from my childhood. It envelops me—I am home at last.

I want to cry. I would take back every evil deed, if only I could go home, but I need only listen to the murmur of the hospital beneath the surface to know it is just an illusion, part of the spell. There is only one way I will be able to leave. The footsteps have stopped. The air has become very still. The door opens with a creak.

He is standing there, just outside. A breeze seems to follow him, and it enters like a whisper. I hear it, petulant and insistent. As he comes close to me, I begin to tremble. For a second I am so cold I fear I may have turned to ice and then I feel the warmth of his arms around me and a slow heat begins to emanate from my body, like a fire that has been lit. As he holds me in his arms I smell the desire in his breath...and then I feel his lips upon mine.

Soft and gentle at first, they taste like sweet wine, rich chocolate, and succulent fruit, all at the same time. I am feasting as I never have before. Before long, his lips become hungry and more demanding. I am consumed by his demands and yield much more quickly than I ever imagined and in doing so, I come alive. I feel my body tingle...the cool sheets beneath my legs and the caress of his hand on my cheek. I want this moment to never end, but it does.

Much to my astonishment, I feel him slowly laying me back down. I want to call out to him, to grab the hem of his shirt. With all my might I pry my eyes open, but it is not the deep blue eyes of my beloved I see. He is already gone.

Instead, it is the watery brown eyes, infested with cataracts that belong to the old woman that greet me...even now they seem to mock me. She looks down at me and smiles, a smile that is both indulgent and humorless.

"I've been waiting for you," she says and I understand too well. I look at her but my sight is blurry. I glimpse a shimmer of blue and smell the scent of old mothballs I know so well from my youth. I give her my sweetest smile.

Later there will be a score to settle, but for right now, I am awake.

The End

THE MOTHER-IN-LAW CURE
Make A Wish Series

BOOK TWO

PROLOGUE
Lahore, Pakistan 1970

This is the type of story that should begin with once upon a time. Once upon a time, she breezed into the city like an icy frost on a hot summer's day. She came and went ruthlessly, like a chill that sets deep inside your lungs and leaves you gasping for air. It was August, and the city of Lahore was sweltering with a heat it had not felt in over fifty years. Society had long fallen asleep beneath the suffocating climate and did not so much as raise a curious glance towards the new stranger. In fact, it was only in the evenings, after sunset, when the severity of the sun's fervor had calmed and a mild breeze passed through stale windows, sleepy courtyards and empty bazaars with the promise of redemption, that people slowly made their way out on to the street, and the city finally breathed its first strangled breath. This was the state of the city when she made her appearance.

It would not be correct to say she was a young woman. Some women are never young. It is written in their destiny, though they may not know it at the time. Certainly, it was the last thing on her mind as she crept across this abandoned part of town. Lost and forgotten were its inhabitants. The town's neglect had made them restless. She could feel them stirring. It wasn't a cold night, yet she began to shiver and then laugh at her own anxiety. With all her power, she willed her body from shaking, her teeth from chattering, her blood from running cold, and walked deeper into the cemetery. The voices urged her forward. When she felt something cold grab her ankle, she stopped. Buried between dust and weeds and rubble, it was barely visible, but there was no denying it; this was the grave that had called out to her. She could hear its whispers; she could feel its anger. It was hungry. She took out a small pouch which contained the tiny heart of a new born chick, so fresh it was still warm, a sprig of cinnamon, the dried petals of a rose, all wrapped together with lock of freshly cut human hair. Hair so soft, so rich…and still exhibiting traces of its fragrant shampoo. Redemption at last, thought Humara and she let out a blood-curdling screech, a laugh that would echo for years to come.

ABOUT THE AUTHOR

Farha Hasan is a Boston-based writer of South Asian descent. She was born and bred in the South Asian community in Toronto and has a degree in business and a passion for books. Her creativity and her love for the written word first took her into advertising and then research. A slave to fiction, Farha has been reading and writing short stories since she first learned to hold a pencil.

www.ingramcontent.com/pod-product-compliance
Lightning Source LLC
Chambersburg PA
CBHW060304260626
47160CB00007B/2502